Midnight in the Pawn Shop

by

DEBORAH K. FRONTIERA

Deborah K. Frontiera

Published by Jade Enterprises

P.O. BOX 841654

Houston TX 77284

In conjunction with Howbrite Solutions, Cokato MN

ISBN 978-1-59346-175-1

Cover design by Designotype Printers, Inc., 22950 Airpark Blvd., Calumet MI 49913 (906) 482-2424

1.   Fiction 2. Fantasy 3. Pawn shops 4. Antiques

b

Introduction

I've been up in the corner of this pawn shop a good many years—rotating automatically between the door and the place where customers stand at the counter. I catch their faces, and sometimes their names. I choose not to talk, but I always think, and record it, so it can all be played back—if anyone ever needed to or wanted to. It hasn't been a boring existence, but usually not all that exciting either. I suppose other security cameras do the same, but I've never met another one to compare my experiences to theirs. If you must have a name, it's Security Camera Model 427, SC427 for short.

Maybe a month ago, there was a tremendous thunder storm—at midnight, of course. One lightning strike was so close it made all the wires in this building sizzle—but I didn't go out because of my battery. Something strange happened after that lightning strike: everything in the place came to life! I suppose they all had some sort of inner life prior to that, could think and remember, watch what happened around them in some way, but never before that night had any of them ever said anything, anytime. At least not on my watch. As the days went by, I began to realize that everything, even objects not in the shop before that night, had had some sort of life inside, and could remember it, as evidenced by the stories they told, but the ability to move

c

around only seemed to happen once they became part of the pawn shop family of things.

That fateful night they all started talking at once. What a cacophony of jumbled sounds that was! They also found they could move around—each in their own way. Finally a handgun yelled at them all and brought some order to the scene. "I don't understand why we can suddenly move and speak to each other, or how long it will last, but let's try to figure out some way to take turns. We've been watching people take turns when they talk, haven't we?" Gun said.

Everyone nodded. A fancy pen put numbers on slips of paper that a scissors from the office drawer cut up from a bunch of packing paper used to wrap fragile objects when they were sold, and anybody who wanted a turn to talk drew one out. They decided there would be one story per night, and if something didn't want to listen, that item could go to the back room to do other things. Any other discussion was cut off as the night ended. All the things realized they must be back in their places by the time the shop owner opened the back door. They agreed they must NEVER talk or move when people were around. An old wind-up clock had arrived at the shop the day before and he said he'd always announce when it was time to start telling stories—as soon as he ended his midnight round of chimes.

I never sleep—always on the job, recording, recording, recording. A neutral party—like that old TV detective I once saw in some reruns on a TV that came into the shop: "Just the facts, Ma'am."

I hadn't planned to share those stories until the day Teapot arrived.

d

Chapter 1

Teapot's Tale

Everyone could see how emotionally wrought she was. Anguished cries came from her pink full-rose mouth and reverberated around the store. Why the humans could not hear her, I'll never know, but everything in the shop remained in place as they had agreed. They didn't want to take a chance on the people knowing they had come to life. So they didn't respond to her right then. I could see she struggled to hold back tears from her tiny pink rose-bud eyes and her bud-nose was a brighter pink. Pale green leaves framed her white porcelain face. Her handle was a spring green curved rose vine, one graceful arm. A larger bud that matched her nose in color sat on her top, easy for a person to lift her lid like a hat. Her white spout reached out like another arm. Her shape was round and motherly.

**

"How can I help you?" the pawn shop owner asked the man carrying Teapot.

"Got this teapot, here. Been in my family for ages, I guess. I want to sell it." His voice couldn't have been more snake-like, unless he magically turned into a cobra.

1

"Okay, let me take a look at it." The shop owner turned the pot over to examine the markings on the bottom. "It's an antique, all right. English, I'm pretty sure, but I'm not all that familiar with this kind of thing. Would you like for me to call an appraiser to get you the best price?"

Like some cheesy cliché character in an old crime movie, the man slid his fingers through long, greasy black hair. "Naw. My mom died. No sisters. My brother's girlfriend didn't want it. I don't want the damn thing either. I'll take whatever you offer."

**

The scream from the pot nearly deafened the closest items on the counter. "Liar! Liar! She wasn't your mother, you murderer!" Why couldn't the humans hear her? Maybe the things didn't need to be so careful when humans were around, but I didn't plan to tell them that idea. Humans might get really creeped out by normally inanimate objects moving around.

**

The pawn shop owner said, "Okay, but without knowing a definite age or value, the best I can offer is $25.00."

"Ahhh! My cups, saucers and I are worth much more than that," the pot wailed, her lilting English accent coming through clearly now.

The young man shrugged, took the cash, slopped a name and other information along with a signature onto a receipt, and stalked out the door.

**

2

The way he looked, I'm willing to bet we'll have a visit from the police before long.

The shop manager set the teapot on the not-for-sale-yet shelf behind the counter. Gradually the pot's wailing subsided into rasping sighs as a nearby vase gave her sympathetic looks. I thought I detected a whisper, "We'll talk later," definitely against all rules of objects when people were around—a rule the teapot obviously didn't know at the time, or was too upset to follow. The anxiety level of every item in the shop increased as the day wore on.

**

Finally, slanted rays of the late-setting summer sun filtered through the dust and burglar bars of the front window. The owner wound up the antique clock—as he did every day when he left—set the shop alarm, and then slipped out the back door quickly before the red light blinked "armed" on the alarm key pad.

Still, everything waited until the old clock struck midnight. Somebody had suggested that time, since by then, it was very unlikely that any people would enter the shop.

**

"Oh, you poor dear," Vase said, sliding closer to Teapot and caressing her with an outstretched side handle. "Whatever happened to you?"

"I hardly know where to start," she said, a dainty sniff coming from her red rosebud nose.

"Start with the murder part," Gun shouted, hopping out from his case. "Then I'll go shoot that bastard!"

3

"Be quiet, Gun," a 35MM camera snapped. "You know you aren't going anywhere and you can't shoot anything without a human to pull your trigger."

Vase turned to Teapot. "There, there, dear. Tell us all about it. We are your friends now."

Teapot sighed. "Please understand, I don't mean to insult your good intentions, but I just can't believe that after all these generations, I must end this way—in a pawn shop, sold for a piddling $25! I'm worth hundreds and hundreds. Why, Abagail Adams once drank tea poured from me at my first mistress's home in Boston. That was back around 1774, when I was brand new. Of course, the day Abagail Adams came, none of us knew that she would one day be one of the nation's First Ladies. We only knew her as our mistress's friend Abagail at the time, but we did know her husband was important in the talk we heard constantly about a revolution on the way. All my little cups and saucers and I were filled with joy at the memory some years later, that the wife of a future president had drunk from one of their sisters and rested her teacake on her brother saucer. I was such a proud mother pot to think that I had poured out tea to her."

It was supposed to be Gun's turn to tell his story that night, but they had all agreed to a rule that the story of a newly acquired item took precedence over the numbering system they had set up. Most of the tools and heavier items nodded in sympathy and clinked away as quietly as they could into the back room to begin the nightly poker game. But the silver set, jewelry items, and other "female" type things gathered around Teapot. TVs and stereos rolled their eyes and prepared for what they probably thought would be a dull history lesson.

Gun started to head for the back room, but stopped and remained by the door, watching the card game begin, but listening to Teapot and ready for action, even though everybody knew he wasn't loaded.

"Go ahead," encouraged Vase. "Tell us everything."

"Well, I continued to live in Boston for many years after that, several generations, actually, and in many different houses. My first mistress passed me to her daughter, who passed me to hers, and on and on. Nothing of real significance happened for a long time. Well, things happened in history, of course, but nothing all that interesting with the families I belonged to—a long string of births, tea parties, marriages, more new babies, deaths and passing me along to a new mistress…I watched ladies' fashions change with each generation."

There was a sigh of relief from the electronics. Being "modern", they weren't much interested in history. Gun remained where he was.

"Go on," urged Vase.

"Well, the various families declined over the years—not so wealthy anymore. I vividly recall one day when the lady of the house had a terrible argument with her husband because he didn't want her to go on some march carrying a sign she had made saying that women should have the right to vote. She won the argument and some months later (as a result of her, and many other suffragettes' work, all across the country) I remember she had a grand tea party celebrating with several friends after they had gone and cast their first votes in the next general election.

"The last old house in which I lived in Boston reverted to the bank that held the mortgage about a decade later—after the crash of 1929—so sad, so sad a day was that. My cups, saucers, and I were carefully wrapped in old newspapers and stored away in a box by that courageous mistress. The box bumped around in the back of an old car while she and her husband traveled around searching for work and a place to live.

5

"A couple of times, he suggested that I be sold—so you see I've come close to this predicament before—but my mistress said, 'Over my dead body will you sell that family heirloom!' and that was the end of that discussion. When I was finally unpacked, they were in a miserable hovel, but I had an honored place on a high shelf where I watched everything that went on. My mistress's husband finally did find a job, and life got better for them. I was so relieved when a baby girl was born—late in life for that couple, and quite a surprise and blessing by what they both said; I knew then that my future was assured."

"Was that here in this city?" Vase asked.

"Yes, it was. And when that baby girl grew up, she chose a good husband and they lived in a bigger house. My cups, saucers, and I were no longer used for tea—seems they drink mostly iced tea here—but I was always honored with a place on a high shelf and treated with utmost dignity. Mothers always told their daughters the story about how I once poured out tea for Abagail Adams and that mother did, too. They were proud of my legacy. Times were good in that generation. But in the next generation there were only boys! No daughter to carry me on. When that lady died, I was given to the wife of the eldest son. But she understood me and was good to me, and they had a daughter.

"Unfortunately, that daughter had poor taste in men. She ran off with a real loser—or at least that's what my lady called him, or 'that damned hippie'. She kept trying to get them to break up, but my young mistress packed me up with a few other things one night and jumped into the hippie's car. He had terribly long hair and said, 'Hey, man,' a lot. He smoked weird-smelling cigarettes that he rolled himself, and my—I just can't call her a lady—smoked them, too. They lived in a dilapidated old trailer on some farm they called 'The Commune' out in the middle of a forest where they grew the stuff they smoked. I was so afraid for the baby girl they had.

"One day, that man picked me up and said, 'What's with this old Teapot?' That Missy (I'd taken to calling her Missy, because Mistress just didn't fit) surprised me by saying, 'It's been in my family for generations. Grandma told me some crazy story about some family from Boston that served tea to Abagail Adams once—if you want to believe it.' The man set me back down carefully with a seemingly thoughtful, 'Hm.' So, I still had some respect; at least she had remembered the story.

"Anyway, when their daughter grew up, her choice in a husband was no better than her mother's—maybe even worse. They actually laughed about it and called themselves 'bum magnets.' But I was passed down a few years ago to another daughter whose choice in men was the worst of all. At least she never married that crook. But he hit her constantly and she had no courage to leave! I just don't understand that. After such a long line of women who lived through so many ups and downs, trials and travails, it was discouraging to have such an insecure owner. At least those before her had kept trying. Maybe it was that son and his wife. Maybe they just didn't get the right traits passed on to them, because it was never the same after that generation with no girls. I could never call any of my owners from that time on 'Mistress'."

*

It was interesting to me that for all her Britishness at the beginning of her tale, Teapot's voice sounded more and more American as the story progressed. I'm not sure why, but I noted the change and on successive nights, her voice varied in the same way, as if she couldn't quite make up her mind whether she was English or not. I'm not trying to be critical, just observant.

7

**

Teapot began to shake and cry. Vase and the jewelry items joined in a circle to comfort her.

"Was that abusive man the one who brought you here?" Vase asked.

Teapot nodded and broke down weeping again. There was a rustle of, "There, there," and, "You're safe now." And, "Tell us what happened."

Gun's expression grew angry. He cocked himself since he could do that much.

Teapot sniffed. Vase touched a tissue to Teapot's red rose nose.

"He was in a drunken rage. He reached up to the shelf where my cups and saucers and I sat. He grabbed a cup and threw it at her! It hit her in the head and crashed! My little daughter crashed on the floor and Missy's head was bleeding.

"She screamed and ran toward me and the rest of the set shouting, 'No, no, please, not those! They're valuable; they're valuable!' I was in shock, but still glad to see that she cared enough to defend me. But he was so drunk and angry. He pushed her down. She crawled to the corner, trying to cover her head with her arms while he threw all the rest of my little cups at her, and then the saucers. Each time they crashed against her—their crash their cry of death—she bled in some new spot. It was like he was torturing her. She slumped to the floor, crying and begging for him to stop.

"I felt so helpless. All my little cups and saucers—all eight of each—were gone. He reached for me! Oh, please don't make this the end of me! I thought. Luckily, he was out of breath and had to stop for a minute. From somewhere, Missy gathered strength. She got up and staggered toward me, grabbed me, and hugged me to her heart."

Gun ambled over to the group as quietly as he could.

Teapot was crying again and it took several minutes for her to calm down.

"They'll get that bastard!" Gun said with a swagger. "You'll see. I was FBI you know—they'll find a clue leading here and catch that guy. Then you might be returned to your owner. You'll see."

Finally, Teapot spoke, "Then that monster of a man picked up a baseball bat and hit her with it! She crumpled to the floor and didn't move. Her arm loosened around me and I rolled to the floor. He looked at her and grunted. He took a shower, packed a suitcase, picked me up and brought me here. What is to become of me?"

Vase caressed Teapot with an outstretched handle. "I'll tell you what's to become of you," she said. "You'll grow strong again with all of us here. And once you've been appraised— because that is why you were over on that high shelf, not with the rest of us that are for sale—you'll begin another legacy with a new family that will appreciate who you are. That's what."

The light of a new day came into the sky. Soon the key clicked in the back door. Everyone hustled into their day places before the owner's fingers did their daily dance over the alarm key pad.

Chapter 2

Broken Record

No new items came in the next day, but several jewelry items and some antique books were sold—stories that would never be heard. Those books had been around for months and months, but never spoke up. Maybe the lightning sizzle didn't affect them. Maybe they couldn't talk, but had to be read. Whatever the reason, they never told the stories inside of them. The usual listeners turned to Gun, as it was his turn.

**

"Come on, Gun," 35MM encouraged, "I can't wait to hear about all the bad guys you always hint at, but never tell about when we are playing cards." 35MM listened or played cards depending on who was telling the story.

There had been some evenings when Gun would start to brag during the card game, but a rude digital game who never participated in the stories had cut him off with, "If you're going to tell stories, go in the front room! You're breaking my concentration."

"Yes, and that stuff about the FBI agent who owned you," Exercise Bike put in.

11

"I got too much to say for one night," Gun said, "so somebody else can go instead. Hey, 33 RPM, isn't your number next? How about you?"

"No, no, no, I can't, I can't," Record said over and over and over.

**

He had never actually drawn a number. Something had just handed him one. I remember he tried to refuse, but couldn't get the words out.

**

Gun tapped him and said, "Sure you can. Whose signature is that on your jacket?"

Record sighed, "It's really hard, really hard, really hard …" he stuttered over and over.

"What's hard?" Vase asked, her eyes full of her usual sympathy. She touched him, too.

"I'm broken, broken, broken, scratched, scratched …"

Gun tapped him again.

"The signature, it's a former Beatle, a former Beatle, a former Beatle …"

This went on for a while. Several items slipped away quietly. Vase urged him to continue with another tap.

"Which Beatle?" she asked.

Finally, the Gun and Vase figured out that a simple touch helped Record speak without repeating himself endlessly. So they took turns tapping him gently until he completed his story.

**

I'll sum it up, rather than include all the repetition and taps:

12

Back in 1970, when John Lennon released his later famous album, Imagine, he autographed a few of the jackets and gave them to selected radio stations for promotion. One of those stations put the copy up as a contest prize. Record's original owner was the winner. That winner loved the album, and John Lennon, so much that he played the record almost nonstop night and day. He usually sang along with it, too. Record emphasized that those were his and his owner's happiest days.

But the same music, over and over, can be nauseating to others who must listen unwillingly. Such was the case for the woman who lived in the apartment next door—sharing the wall where the stereo sat. Of course, the neighbor only heard the base notes humming through the wall, on and on, and on, and on, and on... thum, thum, thum, thum-de-dum-dum, thum, thum, thum, thum-de-dum-dum...until she was nearly insane. Record's repetitions at that point in the story made quite an effect and I think everything could understand the neighbor's later actions.

**

She knocked on Record Owner's door and politely asked him to give her a break, or at least turn down the volume. He promised to turn it off after 10 p.m. each night. He managed to keep that promise for ONE day. Subjected to the continued onslaught, the neighbor knocked on the door again. But this time she wasn't so polite.

She stormed across the tiny living room, pulled the needle across Record as he was playing.

"ZRRRRRIIIIIIPPPPP!" Record screamed in agony as the needle tore a gash across that whole side.

"There!" the neighbor screamed, "Now YOU listen to it over and over and over again!" and stomped out.

Record was never the same. The scar was permanent.

Now here, one must recall that 33RPM stands for 33 revolutions per minute—or a turn of the record about every two seconds. Every time the needle hit the scratch, it would jump back a groove and repeat itself—ad nauseam.

Record Owner tried to listen to the precious notes again but all he could hear was: "Imaging ther — blip—imagine ther— blip—imagine ther— blip …"

He tried ticking the record to get it to the next line: "'E's no heav — bli p—'es no heav— blip—'es no heav—blip …"

Record Owner ranted and screamed for a long time. Then he sadly removed Record from the stereo and gave him a place of honor on top of a book shelf—in revered silence.

Then Record Owner got angry. He contacted the police to have the woman charged with vandalism. After talking to the woman and hearing her side of the story, the police reported the story to the D.A, who declined to press charges. The D.A told Record Owner this was a civil rather than a criminal matter. Record Owner muttered for days and then gathered the courage to go down to the court house and file a civil suit, acting as his own attorney.

Record stated his owner acted like a fool the day he showed Record to the judge on the case. Record saw the judge roll his eyes more than once. Some of the jury shook their heads or put their thumbs and first fingers on either side of the bridges of their noses, rubbing gently. That was the only day Record appeared in court, so he couldn't say anything about how the case went from then on.

It turned out that the woman neighbor was not the only person in the apartment building who had been irritated by the constant playing of Record. The other tenants banded together with her, found out there was an "excessive noise" ordinance in that city and sued Record Owner for violating that ordinance—also in a civil case because the D.A wouldn't prosecute Record Owner, just as she didn't pursue charges against the neighbor for vandalism. Record told everyone about the look of total shock and surprise when an officer knocked on his owner's door and served him with notice that he was being sued. He continued to hear about the progress of the cases from the various phone calls and visits to the apartment that followed.

The first civil jury found against Record Owner in the vandalism case. The second civil jury found for the other tenants. By the time the man paid off all the court costs in both cases, and the lawyer he had decided to hire to defend him in the noise ordinance case, Record Owner was dead broke and evicted for back rent.

**

If you ask me, it was all a lot of brouhaha over something that could have been handled by all the people involved showing each other a little bit of consideration—but people are often strange creatures when it comes to exercising basic common sense.

**

"Where is that man now?" Vase inquired.

"I have no, I have no, I have no …" (tap) "idea," Record replied.

Gun spoke up. "I wonder why that man didn't just go buy another copy of Imagine and put the new record in the old jacket, or just play the unscratched side."

Record shrugged. Then he stuttered through telling how his owner wandered around that city aimlessly, begging for money for food—which he usually spent on cheap booze—living in parks and under freeway bridges, clinging to Record even though he had nothing on which to play him. He told us his owner had always seemed "a few sandwiches short of a picnic" (which it took several times for him to say straight), but he really "went off the deep end" as some people say, after the court cases. One day, he handed the record over to this pawn shop owner, Mr. Garcia, who happened to be visiting that city. Record Owner sold Record to Mr. Garcia for a few hundred bucks, and he has been on the highest shelf in this store ever since.

The day after Record told everyone that story, a customer entered the pawn shop and wanted to buy Record. He offered the shop owner a huge sum. The owner's reply stunned every item in the store. "Sorry, friend, neither that record, nor its jacket, are for sale. It's the best of my personal collection. I keep it on display because I'm proud to own it."

"May I ask how you acquired it?" the customer said.

"You may ask, but I won't tell you. I plan to pass it on to my musician grandson when he comes of age."

The customer and Mr. Garcia talked back and forth for a while as the customer continued to try to convince Mr. Garcia to sell him Record. The customer even said he didn't care about the scratch.

"I don't care about the scratch, either," Mr. Garcia said.

"Well, if you ever change your mind, here's my card," the man said.

**

He looked around the shop and right up at me! I had just finished a sweep of the shop and swung back to aim my

16

lens at the counter again. There was a look in his eye that told me I'd better watch out at night in case he tried to break in.

ChaptER 3

A Simple BikE Story

The next night, there was a lot of plain conversation before any storytelling even began. Just a jumble of voices until nearly 4 a.m. Then Exercise Bike reminded Gun, "It's your turn tonight." The others nodded in agreement.

"Listen!" Gun shouted. "I'll tell my story when I'm damn good and ready." He pointed his barrel at Exercise Bike in a threatening manner, even though everyone knew there were no bullets in him. "You tell us your story."

"Uh, uh, not much to tell, really."

35MM glared at Gun, and then turned to Exercise Bike. "Don't mind him. He's just a blowhard."

Teapot frowned at Gun and then said to Exercise Bike, "I'd enjoy hearing your story, though."

Gun glared back at Teapot, but backed away.

"Yes, do tell," Diamond Ring rang out, rolling over from the jewelry case.

"Okay, but I warn you, it's not exciting in any way. I won't be offended if anyone chooses to leave."

Instead of leaving, half a dozen items that usually played cards came over to listen.

"I'm not an antique," he began, "or valuable at all. I'm not

19

even that old. Just two years ago, I was manufactured, boxed, and delivered to a chain retail store. I spent several months in my box in the back of the store, then more time—I didn't keep track—sitting in the store display area. She, my only owner, looked at me. It was an 'after Christmas' sale and my price had been slashed. She said I'd be her New Year's Resolution.

"A store employee carried me out to her car and managed to fit me in a tight hatch-back, tying down the hatch-back door for her with a piece of rope. When she got to her apartment, she stood for a moment staring at it, wondering how she would get it out by herself.

"The guy from across the hall sauntered down the sidewalk at just that point. 'Hi, I'm Tom. Remember me from the laundry room? What's a gorgeous girl like you need with an exercise bike? Can I help you get that out of your car?'

"She smiled. 'I sit all day in an office. I want to get in shape. I'm Amber, and, yes, I could use a hand. This thing is kind of heavy.'

"Why they had talked in the laundry room but not exchanged names, I don't know, but Tom wiggled and jiggled that bike out of Amber's car and carried it easily into her apartment. Once I was in and placed in a corner of the bedroom, Tom hung around, hoping to be invited to stay, I think.

"'Can I pay you for your time?' Amber asked.

"He took her hand gently. 'For My Lady Amber? Never,' he said with a low bow. She smiled, and as gently as he'd taken her hand, slipped her hand out of his.

"'Well, anyway, thanks.'

"He smiled and said, 'See you around sometime?'

"'Maybe,' my new owner said.

"Tom left with a long last glance at Amber.

"The first month of my relationship with Amber was wonderful! Every evening when she got home from work, she'd stretch out, then get on and ride me. Then off to the shower, followed by a glass of white wine while she fixed her dinner. She didn't ride me very long at first, but over time, she rode longer and longer. I felt so excited each time she increased speed and incline, toughening up her muscles. The feel of her butt in my saddle ..."

Exercise Bike sighed. His audience remained quiet.

"Our honeymoon ended though. She skipped a night here and there to go out with her friends. She still rode me regularly, but now it was every other night. One Friday night, she came home humming and went straight to the shower. She threw her damp towel onto me! And put on her best dress and platform shoes. Who should knock on the door half an hour later? Tom!

"Pretty soon she was seeing HIM every night and I was covered with smelly, dirty laundry!"

Diamond Ring looked at him curiously and said, "I think I know how you feel. What happened then?"

"Well, Amber started spending more and more time with Tom. Pretty soon she was packing up her stuff and moving across the hall into his apartment—supposedly to 'save money on rent.' HA! Naturally, there wasn't enough room for me in Tom's place, so…here I am. Told you there wasn't much to say."

Several items said a quiet "sorry" and shuffled off to other activities. But Diamond Ring looked long and hard at Exercise Bike. "Their names were Amber and Tom?"

"Yes, why?"

"Well, a 'Tom' bought me for a girl named Amber who lived with him in a small apartment! You don't suppose it could be the same couple, do you?"

"Maybe. Do you remember the name of the apartment complex? I caught the name on the sign when Amber first brought me home. I could see it through the gap in the open hatchback. The rope keeping the hatchback down didn't block any of the words. I lived at Crystal Shores. Was that where your Tom and Amber lived?"

"Oh! My! God! Yes!"

Then Diamond Ring broke into tears—to be comforted by Teapot and Vase, of course.

"Oh, for crying out loud!" Gun said, sauntering off in a huff.

**

We all heard the click of the key in the lock on the back door. Everyone, including me, would have to wait until the next night to hear the rest of that story.

Chapter 4

Tom, Amber, and Diamond Ring

Many of the items hung around to listen to Diamond Ring's story as soon as the old clock struck midnight. The look on Gun's face said loud and clear that he was relieved not to be called upon. They seemed to have forgotten about the numbers they'd drawn.

**

Exercise Bike came right to the point. "So Amber dumped Tom, too?"

Diamond Ring chuckled. "Well, I wouldn't put it quite that way. Of course, I don't know what it was like right at the beginning of their relationship because I was still locked in a case at the jewelry store. Bike, what time of the year was it when Amber moved into his apartment?"

"I recall that the calendar was on the April page," Bike replied.

**

I don't know why, but it always surprises me when things don't notice time passing. I always know the exact day and the time as well—all my tapes are date/time stamped. That's an important feature in the event that someone tries to break into the shop. It's also important to police officers who might want to try to identify someone trying to sell stolen merchandise to the pawn shop.

**

"Then there are several months we don't know about," Ring said. "It was in September that the two of them came into the jewelry store, all smiles and stars in their eyes..."

The jewelry items, Vase, Teapot, and several pieces of silver all sighed while some of the power tools groaned and excused themselves. Gun hung around by the door between the back room card game and the show room (like the night of Teapot's story) as if he didn't know what he wanted to do. He had done that a lot lately.

"I was not the most expensive ring in the showcase, nor was I the cheapest," Ring began. "Amber and Tom both looked at the prices—Amber's eyes drifted toward the larger settings and Tom's toward the smaller ones.

"'May I help you?' asked the jeweler.

"'Yes,'" they both said at the same time, and then laughed. Amber tried on several—from the expensive end—with Tom saying each time that the ring didn't seem quite 'you', meaning Amber, of course. Then he picked up some delicate rings from the other end of the case—and Amber said that each of those that they weren't quite right either. Gradually, they worked their way to the middle and to me! Amber didn't seem perfectly happy with me, but she liked me better than the small ones. Tom tapped his fingers on the counter and said something about asking for some 'overtime'. Finally, I was acceptable to both.

Tom pulled out a credit card and signed the sales receipt. He slipped me on Amber's finger and said, 'Now it's official. I can't wait for you to meet my parents at Christmas.'

"They wove their arms around each other and we all went out the door.

"Everything seemed perfect at first. Those two were so in love with each other. Amber looked at my sparkle frequently and showed me off to everyone in the office where she worked as a mid-level manager. All the women employees ooohed and aaahhhed and congratulated her.

"Then the holidays arrived. Tom and Amber took a trip in his car to a very small town where his parents lived. Even though the house was modest otherwise, the Christmas lights on that house sparkled even more than I did! Tom and Amber had decided not to put up a tree or lights in their tiny apartment because they would be gone anyway.

"Of course, there were all the usual hugs and introductions and 'welcome to our family' and 'when will the wedding be?' type things said. 'Oh, we haven't set a date yet, Mom,' Tom had said. Amber gave Tom a strange look as she was shown to the spare bedroom and Tom took his suitcase to his old room. Tom put a finger to his lips and glanced at both parents quickly. Apparently, he had not told his parents about the two of them living together."

A soft murmur went around the items listening, as if they could sense what might be coming.

"During dinner on Christmas Eve, Tom's parents asked the typical questions about Amber: what do you do; where are you from?...Amber told them about her manager's job, emphasizing that she was up for a promotion. She seemed evasive on the subject of her family, saying only, 'Well, I'm not really close with my family.'

25

"Of course, Tom's parents both said, 'Well, we're happy that Tom has brought you into ours! Wait until you meet all the others tomorrow.'

"I felt Amber's hand grow very tense as more and more aunts, uncles, and cousins piled into the house carrying presents and dishes of food around noon on Christmas Day. Everybody hugged her, welcomed her, and you'd think she'd have been glad, seeing as how she said she didn't have much family. But instead she grew quieter. Her smile seemed to be painted on her face—or maybe glued—as she kept saying that she'd never remember all the names.

"Then one of Tom's brothers asked him when he planned to move back to their small town. 'They're hiring down at the plant again. Bet you could make more than that place in the city.' And Tom said he'd check into that as soon as he could. Amber's smile disappeared and her eyes grew wide at that comment.

"The conversation continued to bubble on about who else had gotten married, who was having a baby, what older person in the town had passed on…Amber put her smile back on and remained quiet. Several girl cousins mentioned doing a wedding shower for Amber. 'Oh, it's a bit soon to plan that,' was all she said.

"At one point Tom asked his oldest brother if he would be his Best Man. 'Honored,' was the reply, and, 'Hey, you know the Jones' place just came on the market—perfect newly-wed home.' He jabbed Tom in the ribs. Amber fidgeted and ran her fingers through her hair.

"She did smile and say thank you to the many small gifts given to her—a tiny bottle of perfume, a scarf (really garish but she managed to say it was 'unique') a gift card for a discount store ('will come in handy'). Meanwhile, Tom was absolutely beaming away, laughing with his brothers and cousins. When the day was finally over, and Amber went to bed—alone in the spare room—she flopped down on the bed and whispered to herself, 'What the heck have I gotten myself into?' I didn't know what to think."

By this point, most of the male items had drifted away. The female items were saying the "oh…so sad…not well suited …" kinds of things.

"Amber lingered in the bedroom the next morning, listening to laughter in the kitchen as Tom and his parents ate breakfast. 'Isn't Amber up yet?' his mother remarked. 'She seems like such a sweet girl. Awfully quiet, though, but I expect you'll bring out her best.'

"Tom started to say, 'She's never up early' but it came out, 'She's nev—I mean, I think she was really tired from all the excitement yesterday. I'll go knock on her door.'

"Amber groaned as she heard his footsteps in the hall. 'Hon, you awake yet?'

"A soft moan, 'I'll be right there.'

"Pretty soon, she was in the kitchen nibbling on pancakes and bacon, engaged in small talk. They loaded up their suitcases and headed back for the city.

"Tom bubbled, 'So, what do you think of my family? They really like you! How about a July wedding?'

"Amber seemed cautious. 'Uh, Tom, were you serious about living there?'

"'Sure. Why? I mean, since you never mention your family, I just thought that …'

"Amber took a deep breath. 'There's a reason I don't talk about my family.'

"Tom pressed the subject he'd always avoided. 'Well, I think it's time you did, Amber.'

"She huffed—loudly—and finally unloaded. 'Because I don't have a family! My mother was a drug addict. She didn't even know who my father was, so that line is blank on my birth certificate! Imagine telling that to your small town crowd. I haven't seen her since I was five—don't even know if she's alive or not. I grew up in a bunch of different foster homes—never part of any, really. I aged out at eighteen working in a fast food joint, clawed my way through junior college on scholarships. Yeah, your parents would really like to hear that. You couldn't even tell them we were living together. I've worked my way up in the business world—determined to make something of myself, by myself. I've earned both my B.S. and M.S. in business through online classes—with student loans and a couple of grants from women's groups. I'm working my ass off to pay back the loans—unlike some who just dump their loans unpaid. I'm just beginning to build my life! Why would I want to live in a small town like that?' Her voice had risen with every sentence she spoke.

"Tom interrupted, 'But, Amber, sweetheart, you will have a family now. My parents won't care about your past! I didn't tell them we lived together because, well, they are sort of old-fashioned about that stuff. Believe me! They already love you—just like I do.'

"Amber seemed to settle down a little. She whispered a 'sorry' for blowing up and both were quiet for a while. They did talk more about their future in the weeks that followed—with Amber always mentioning the soon-to-be promotion and liking the city, while Tom emphasized that he'd live anywhere as long as he could be with her and if she didn't want to, they wouldn't have to visit his family that much. But it was the beginning of the end. I could feel it every time Amber twisted me around her finger."

Ring stopped talking for a moment. The other jewelry items circled around her in sympathy. Vase and Teapot patted her with their handles.

Ring sighed. "The day Amber got her promotion, I almost thought it might still work. Tom was thrilled for her. 'So where is the company sending you?' he asked. Amber looked at the floor and said, 'New York.' Tom seemed to shrivel like an old balloon. 'Oh, well, I guess it won't be too hard for me to find a job there.' He put his arms around her, but she just stood there, not hugging him back.

"Tom always had to leave for work earlier than Amber did. The next day, she packed her suitcase and walked out the door. She left me on the table with a note:

'Dear Tom,

I never meant to hurt you and I'm sorry. You deserve someone who really loves you. I'm not what you need. You should go home to one of those cute small town girls.

Goodbye,

Amber'

Even the back room was quiet—for once. The only sound was the occasional distant hum of a car on the near-by freeway.

Bike finally broke the silence. "So, she dumped me for Tom, and then dumped Tom for New York. Figures."

Teapot patted Ring again and asked, "What did Tom do when he found you and the note?"

"He just stared at me for the longest time. Then he read the note, crumpled it up and tossed it. He talked to himself about giving notice at work and going home, and that's what he did. He packed up his stuff, and the last thing he did before heading out of town was to sell me here."

Vase, in her usual way, said, "I think Amber just didn't know how to love because she didn't get the love she needed as a child. I'm sure that very soon, you'll go on the hand of a young woman who loves her man as much as he loves her."

**

Before anything could say another word, we were all startled by a crash and the back door splintered and flew opened.

Chapter 5

Break In

Hoodie flopped over his head and covering part of his face, the man ran through the back room and into the showroom. I swung around trying to catch his face, but the hood blocked a clear view. I had a bet with myself that it was the man who had tried to buy Record. The thief climbed onto the glass-topped jewelry counter and reached for Record up on the highest shelf—confirming my suspicion. Everything in the shop froze, half in fear and half in shock. We'd never been broken into as long as I've been here. Also, everything not in its place knew they should not move when anyone, even a criminal, could see.

**

Gun kept opening his mouth and closing it. He wanted to act but held back for some reason. The thief's right foot was right next to where Vase and Teapot sat on the counter where they had been for Diamond Ring's story. With a desperate look on her face, Teapot rolled over into the man's foot, knocking him off balance.

31

The thief grabbed for the next lower shelf in an attempt to steady his position. Then Vase reached out an arm and pushed his foot harder. Down he came! Teapot and Vase had all they could do to roll away before they would have been crushed beneath him.

The courage of those two got everyone else into action. Several items on that second-to-the-top shelf landed on the man once he was down and bounced off. Hammer jumped out of his tool box in time to join Gun. They both gave the thief a good CONK on the head. The thief slumped to the floor.

Gun looked up. "You okay, Record?"

"Ye...ye...yes. I'm...fine."

"Great move, Teapot," Vase said.

"You, too!"

"What do we do now?" Diamond Ring asked.

In his usual way, Gun took charge, "Well, we should just get ourselves back where we belong and wait for the police to arrive. This fool tripped the silent alarm when he broke in."

Vase started to ask what a silent alarm was, but she was cut off by the sound of wailing sirens. Every item froze wherever they had landed.

Two police officers, guns drawn, entered cautiously through the broken-down back door. First one, then the other scooted across the back room and froze in place a moment on either side of the doorway to the showroom, keeping behind the wall. They gave each other a glance and then one shouted out, "Police! FREEZE!" while the other whipped round into the sales area, ready to fire if needed.

"CLEAR!" the officer in the show room said, lowering his weapon and shaking his head at the scene.

The thief lay on the floor in front of the glass jewelry counter—out cold. Gun and Hammer lay on each side of his head. Vase and Teapot lay on their sides on top of the counter. Diamond Ring had never been so flat against top of the glass case. Exercise Bike was in the middle of the room, not in his usual place by the front window, because he had come over for the story earlier. Record, the object the thief had wanted to abscond with, sat in his usual place on the high shelf. The shelf right below Record, which the thief had tried to grab for balance, lay smashed on the floor. All the items on that shelf, and those that had tried to jump the thief, lay scattered around the floor. It seemed almost a miracle. NOTHING was broken except the shelf!

"What the …?" the police officer said. He reached out to the thief's neck and checked for a pulse. "He's not dead."

The other officer joined him. "Owner's on his way. Let's cuff this guy while he's still out. Better call for an ambulance, though."

The two officers cuffed the thief, pulling his hood back as they did so. It WAS the man who had tried to buy Record.

A low groan announced that the thief had regained consciousness. His eyes opened with a wild look. "Get off me! Get off me!" he yelled.

"Nothing's on you, man," one of the officers said. "You're under arrest for breaking and entering."

"They're alive! That teapot tripped me!" the guy went on.

**

Oh, oh, were we all found out?

**

"Yeah, sure," the second officer said, rolling his eyes. He looked toward his partner. "I'll get the breath test gear."

The first officer nodded. They thought he was drunk. That was a relief! Once they'd made him breathe into the little tube, they hustled him outside—to the back of the patrol car, I assumed.

Not long after that, Mr. Garcia arrived. The second officer was taking pictures when he walked in. Mr. Garcia put his hands on his head and groaned when he saw the mess. "Let me finish up these photos and then you'll need to check and see what all is missing or damaged," the officer said.

Mr. Garcia stood still, just looking around for a few minutes. Then the officers asked him to go outside and take a look at the guy they'd caught.

"That's the dude who wanted to buy my prized record," Garcia said when they all came back in. "But look at this mess and the record is right up there!" He pointed up to Record.

"Looks like he was trying to reach it," one officer observed. "Must have lost his balance."

"Yeah, that makes sense. And he might have decided to take this gun. But why is this exercise bike dragged over here? And why would he get a hammer out of that tool box?"

"Maybe he rummaged around looking for the record and tried to use the bike to get up to the shelf," one officer suggested. "Or maybe we've got a nut case on our hands. He was yelling something crazy about that teapot tripping him." He followed his statement with a hardy laugh.

The other officer looked up at me. "Well, we could look on the security tape to be sure."

*

I could see everything looking up at me. I could tell they were worried that all their actions would have been recorded.

**

Mr. Garcia got a ladder, climbed up, took out my tape pack, put it in the VCR next to a small TV and turned it on.

Lots of eyes were on that screen—and not just human eyes either.

There was the sound of the crash, and then footage of the thief entering the room, looking right up at Record, reaching… and then it went fuzzy. The next clear scene showed the man on the floor and the officers entering.

**

Even I was surprised.

**

"What the heck?" Mr. Garcia said.

"Maybe a bad tape," one officer suggested.

"Well, doesn't really matter," said the other officer. "We've got the guy, thanks to your silent alarm. You'll need to come down to the station as soon as you can to fill out the paperwork to press charges. For now, we'll leave you so you can pick up everything and make a list of the damages and all that."

"Yeah, and call someone to come pronto and put in a new back door," Mr. Garcia said. He shook his head, sighed, and started picking things up.

Chapter 6

Vase Reveals Her Story

It had been quite a day as Mr. Garcia cleaned everything up, checking each piece carefully and putting them back in their places. He was writing notes on a tablet as he did this, still scratching his head occasionally and muttering to himself. He made several phone calls: a contractor friend who arrived in an hour with a new door—a metal one with a metal frame this time; his insurance company; a security company with a request for the best available recording tapes, and, no, he didn't care about the cost; and one of his part-time employees to cover the shop while he went to the police station to file charges against the man who broke in.

**

When the old clock struck midnight, everything in the shop was ready to talk, except me. I kept quiet as usual. Even though I was glad the lives of the items had not been revealed, I was still trying to figure out for myself why the tape had gone fuzzy.

The items talked for quite a while about what had happened. Then somebody said they felt ready for a

37

story. Several others reminded Gun that he had skipped his turn several times.

Gun insisted on passing on his turn again and pointed at Vase, insisting that she tell her story. If I could count all the times I've saved his bullying statements onto digital memory tape ... but Vase's beauty, charm and compassion had made everyone wonder what her story was.

**

"Gun, if you will stop being so cocky, I will tell my story, but only if you promise not to threaten anybody else," Vase said.

"Okay, sorry," Gun muttered. "I won't threaten anybody else, if y'all will just quit trying to make me talk before I'm ready!"

Everyone nodded their agreement to this arrangement. From that night on, items would volunteer, rather than following the pre-set, numbered schedule.

So, Vase began. "My owner, my creator actually, was the loveliest young woman—an artist, a potter. Her work had a wide reputation and sold in many top galleries. I was not supposed to be sold—ever—but was to be a last gift to my creator's young daughter."

Vase stopped and swallowed hard, as though she couldn't bear the thought of what she had to tell. She pointed to the bright orange sun, and the shades of yellow, red and lavender surrounding it that were painted on her.

"I was supposed to be either sunset, or sunrise, and indeed I was both: the sunset of my creator's life, and the sunrise of her daughter's. You see, my creator was dying of cancer when she made me. Into me, she poured all the love she knew she would never be able to give to her daughter—who was only five at that time. The little girl, Anna, watched her mother when she painted the sun on me. 'This is all my love for you,' she told Anna, 'It's all here in the sunrise of your life, warm colors all around you. Hold onto this vase and know I will be in your heart, always.' Anna only stared at me and her mother, not understanding, you see."

**

Every item listening that night—especially Gun—sat as still as if they had been near the altar of a church. Vase's voice was like a melody, and I suppose we all needed the feeling of peace she gave us after the events of the previous night.

**

"All the while she worked on me, that young mother sang a song:

'Abba, Abba Father, you are the potter
I am the clay; the work of your hands.
Mold me, mold me and fashion me
Into the image of Jesus your son,
Of Jesus your son.'"

The clear notes Vase sang rose around the listeners. Tears ran down Teapot's face.

Vase continued, "She sang that song to her daughter every night, too. I could hear her when she tucked the child into bed, since my creator's studio was just downstairs from the child's loft bedroom. The very last thing she did was to scratch the word 'Abba' into my base, to remind her daughter that she, and the Father, would always be in her heart. I am the only piece she did not sign or date, as I was not to be sold."

"I'm sorry to interrupt, Vase," Teapot whispered, "But if you were to be for the little girl, how …?"

Vase's handles shook a tiny bit as she went on, "That last night, she put me in the kiln with several other items. That's how the terrible mix-up began. You see, she never came home again. She died while I was being fired! The kiln was on a timer, of course, and went off when it was supposed to. There were some figurines, another vase, and three bowls. I wondered why we sat in the dark oven, long after we had cooled. I don't know why, but we didn't talk to each other as we do here."

Vase choked on the words as she told everyone that several weeks went by before the kiln was finally opened. "We were lifted out by strangers. Boxes lay all about—some taped shut, some still opened. They were packing up my creator's studio.

"'Look what I found!' one of the packers shouted. 'There are new pieces in this kiln. She must have made these right before her death!' These people were all excited, for my kiln companions and I were apparently some of my potter's most beautiful work. The words 'exquisite colors', 'unique shape', and 'these will bring the highest prices' floated around as we were carefully wrapped and placed in a box. I looked around just before I was covered with packing paper, but I couldn't see Anna anywhere.

"'I'm supposed to be for Anna,' I shouted, but, of course, they could not hear me. The next thing I knew, we were all on display in a huge gallery. We were admired by many over the next couple of weeks. Then, an auctioneer arrived and stood before a crowd of people. One by one, we were held up and offered to the highest bidder.

"Several times, we heard the auctioneer say, 'Come on, folks, all this is for the child's college fund. Who'll give me another $50?' I was the last piece to be sold, and I went to an elderly lady. I wanted to weep—I was supposed to be Anna's special vase.

"The next day, as the elderly lady was looking me over again, she saw the 'Abba' on my bottom. I heard a shriek somewhere between shock and rage. She wrapped me right back up and returned me to the gallery.

"'This piece I bought yesterday is NOT signed! What's this silly Abba on the bottom—that old 80s singing group? This is a fraudulent attempt to sneak an unauthenticated piece of work into that of a wonderful artist. I want my money back!'

"Half of me was relieved, half of me crushed. I was my creator's best work ever—the most vividly colored and glazed, now insulted by this woman. But by returning me, I could be given to Anna!"

Teapot reached out to comfort Vase, as she had once been comforted by that lovely work of art. The shop remained silent.

Vase finally found the strength to continue her story. The gallery owner had been called in. He looked at Vase and assured the woman that he had been present when Vase was packed up from the studio, and knew the potter well. The woman would have none of that, even threatened a lawsuit. So the gallery, not wishing to have their reputation questioned, refunded her money.

"I waited in the gallery back room for years, hoping to be returned to Anna, but it never happened. I didn't even have the smaller satisfaction that the price for me would help Anna when she grew up. I think she would be twenty-something now, but I've lost track of exactly how many years have gone by. The gallery finally sold me for a pittance in a giant 'garage sale' of old, unknown art. I've been shuffled around from one shop or collector to another ever since. But I know, somehow, and I don't know how I know, but Anna will find me—someday."

Teapot moved as close to Vase as she could. "Well, you may not have been able to give a mother's love to Anna, but you certainly have given it to everyone else here, especially me these last few days."

The other items slipped quietly away, leaving Vase and Teapot to comfort each other before the familiar sound of the lock opening on the shop's back door.

Chapter 7

Teapot Leaves Us

A few days later, a uniformed officer walked into the shop. He looked around at all the items, especially the various dishes. I focused on him immediately.

**

"What can I do for you, Officer Daniels?" Mr. Garcia said. "Are you doing a follow-up on my recent break-in?"

"No, this is quite another matter. I'm looking for an item that might match this." He pulled a photograph of some broken cups and saucers from a file folder in his hand.

**

I could see Vase, Teapot and some of the others gasp silently—especially Teapot as she recognized the smashed bodies of her children—but of course, none of the humans noticed this.

**

The owner sighed. "I had a feeling I might have a visit concerning this. It's been a while since I acquired this teapot, but I had some reservations at the time." He reached up and lifted Teapot down from the shelf behind the counter. "I had a feeling the sleaze bag who brought this in might have stolen it because he didn't want to wait for an appraisal."

Officer Daniels measured the diameter of Teapot's bottom and compared it to another photo of several dust-free circles on an otherwise very dusty shelf. Her bottom matched the dust-free circle exactly. Then he compared the pattern of roses on Teapot's side to the roses in the picture of one of the broken cups. "Yup. I'm pretty sure this is the right one. It wasn't 'stolen' as such, but it is evidence in an assault. Going to have to take it with me."

**

The word "assault" as opposed to "murder" caused another silent ruckus among the items for sale. Teapot's eyes about popped out of her rose pattern.

**

The shop owner sighed again. "Oh, well. Glad I didn't pay the guy much for it. Guess I'll have to cancel that appointment with the appraiser."

"Actually, we'd like any information about the seller, too."

"Daniels, you've been in here before. You know I keep accurate records. I don't suppose you can tell me anything about the case? Just curious."

Daniels set down the photos and put both hands on the counter. "You know I'm just a patrol officer on this errand, but here's the story around the station. Young woman was brutally assaulted. Perp probably thought she was dead. A neighbor heard the ruckus, but was afraid to call it in at first. She only called 911 after she saw the perp leave the apartment. Said she'd seen him around before; thought he might be a boyfriend. Young woman was actually alive when investigators arrived! Heard she's in a coma, but they think she'll make it. Detectives are all out running down other leads. That's why they sent me here instead of coming themselves."

Our owner whistled. "So have you arrested the guy?"

"Not yet. Even though the neighbor had seen him around, it was always from the back. She couldn't give a very good description and didn't know his name. The crime scene people got good prints off the broken cups and saucers, but no match in our data bases. Then, after several dead ends, and a second look at the crime scene, somebody spotted the dust-free circles on the shelf. Counting up the broken pieces, sizes of the other circles in the dust, investigators figured there was a piece unaccounted for—likely a teapot since the other circles matched one pieced-together saucer—so I got assigned to search the area pawn shops for it, and here I am. We're actually hoping you'll have some security footage that'll help us ID the guy."

"Yeah, I do. And I'll get you the paper work, too. Be right back."

Officer Daniels placed Teapot carefully in an evidence bag and then wrapped the bag in a cloth to protect it. Then he walked around while he waited, giving absent-minded glances at various items.

**

Mr. Garcia returned from the back room with some papers and a cassette of digital video tape—out of me, I'm proud to say. Nobody ever looks up here in the corner at me or thinks about me except when there's a crime I might have recorded. That's my job as a security

45

*camera, but I never get any thanks for it. Today I'm sure
they were all glad I was on the job, even though nobody
said anything. All those items telling their stories don't
seem to notice me either. I never get asked to join in.
Maybe they don't know I can talk, but that's not my job.
I'm here to record, not talk.*

**

"Here you go," our owner said. "I made a copy of the form the
guy signed for my tax records—another damn loss. Will I get
the security tape back later? I reuse them when I can."

"Don't know for sure. City budget is pretty tight, but there
might be some reward funds from Crime Stoppers if the tape
leads to a conviction. We do appreciate your help, though."

Daniels put the papers and digital tape cartridge in the file
folder and turned to leave.

"Hey, Daniels, if you get a chance, stop back by and let me
know what happens on this one, okay? The guy's probably left
town, or at least left the neighborhood, but if I see him again,
I'll give the precinct a call."

"Appreciate your cooperation. I'll try to stop by if there's
any new development."

**

That night, no one told any stories. They were too busy talking
about Teapot. It was quite a jumble of voices, many talking at
the same time.

"So Teapot's owner is still alive!"

"Yeah, but in a coma—didn't he say that?"

"What will happen to Teapot? Will we ever see her again?"

"Hope they find that man! And string him up."

On and on. It's hard to sort out voices when everybody talks at once.

Gun finally shouted above the din. "Hey, everybody, slow down! One at a time."

**

Everyone looked at him, and then waited. I guess they all figured he'd let them know all the answers.

**

"Look," Gun said. "If Teapot's owner wakes up, and ends up okay, then Teapot will probably be returned to her after this guy's trial is over—assuming they find him. If they find him guilty, he'll go to jail for a pretty long time—depends on what the jury decides and a lot of other stuff—like if it's his first offense, or if the young woman has really serious injuries, and if she even swears out a complaint against him. It'll be a long drawn-out mess. But one thing I can say for sure: we probably won't see Teapot back here again."

"Why not?" asked Exercise Bike.

"Because she'll be logged into evidence, then sit on some shelf in a box in the evidence room until the trial, if there ever is one. And if there isn't a trial, she'll go back to her owner."

"And we might never know," sighed Vase.

"That's right," Gun said, sitting down on his butt.

**

Everyone sighed. While relieved that there might be some justice, they'd lost a friend and didn't know whether it would be a happy, or at least hopeful, outcome. A depressing day and night. So often I've wondered why

47

it takes SO long for anything to happen with justice in the world of people. Seems to me it ought to be a fairly simple thing, but no, people drag it on for months and sometimes years by the scuttlebutt I hear from day to day.

Chapter 8

Camera's Adventures

There was nothing anyone could do about the whole situation with Teapot, so the next night, the items gathered to resume sharing their stories. There was an awkward moment of quiet as they all waited for someone to volunteer.

**

With a click of his shutter, 35MM Camera said, "Well, I'm okay talking about myself tonight, if anyone wants to listen."

The usual crowd circled around him, nodding whatever they had for a head.

"I'm a really specialized model," 35MM began. "I can zoom in on something really far away and do freeze-action type shots. That's good for wildlife photographers, and that's what my owner was. Oh, what adventures we had!"

"Was it ever dangerous?" asked Gun.

"Sometimes. But not always. Other times it was almost boring—tedious waiting for some animal or bird to show up. But let me start at the beginning. My owner's parents gave me to her. It was her college graduation and she had just gotten a job as a photojournalist for a wildlife preservation group. She was happy; her parents were happy; I was happy.

"Her first assignment was to photograph some baby bald eagles in a nest way at the top of a huge pine tree in a northern forest. I can tell you first hand, that mama eagle wasn't too thrilled when my owner started climbing that tree! She looped a wide belt—the kind like you see lumbermen wear when they climb up tall trees—around her and the tree. She would dig these spikes strapped to her boots into the tree bark and pull up, then sort of jump the belt, step up with the spikes, over and over. Every time the eagle dived at us, my owner would stop her climb and curl up as tightly as she could against the tree trunk. First the mother eagle, then the father eagle would dive and screech at us. She was wearing a heavy leather jacket and leggings, and a helmet to protect her if the eagles decided to peck or rip with their sharp talons or beak. She would talk softly and wait, then resume her climb. I hung from her neck, scared half to death.

"I don't know how she did it, but she finally gained the trust of that pair of eagles. She got right up to the branch where the nest was! She didn't climb out onto the limb, though, just stayed near the tree's trunk. Click, click, click went my shutter. A whole roll of film shot off! It took some careful maneuvering for her to put the exposed roll of film into her backpack and reload me with another roll.

"Then something even more amazing happened. She looked out and one of the parent eagles made a dive toward the lake near the tree. Came up with a good-sized fish! The parent eagle returned to the nest, and right in front of us, ripped up that fish to feed those young eagles. Click, click, click… another roll of film used! I captured both the fish catch and the feeding! The parent eagles didn't even object much when she finally got close enough to the nest to put tiny ID bands (that the conservation group she worked for had given her) around the eaglets' legs so they could be tracked later. Those bands were curious things. They clamped around the eaglet's leg and were loose enough to allow for growth, but couldn't fall off because of the little eagle's talons."

The excitement in his voice was contagious. Not a single item left the gathering. Everyone stretched up as much as they could to listen.

"The young photographer's employers were really pleased with her work—called her the 'eagle whisperer'. The pictures and her story ended up being a feature article in the organization's magazine. Well, you can imagine how many job offers she got after that! She did do some freelance work for other outfits, but she liked the people she worked for, so she stayed with them and did many other assignments.

"We photographed giraffes and elephants in Africa; caught a lion hunting antelope with my night-vision feature; recorded the care and feeding of baby chimpanzees with their mothers... The wildlife organization once said, 'You're not just an 'eagle whisperer'; you're our 'wildlife whisperer.'

"Of course, it wasn't always fun and games. One time, we sat hanging by ropes from a cliff for several boring hours waiting for some endangered big-horned mountain sheep that never did show up. But the worst time was when a plastic piece of my lens cover cracked from the arctic cold waiting for a mother polar bear—that also didn't show. My owner had to give up when her fingers were too numb to operate my shutter. She barely made it back to her camp and lost the end of her left pinky finger to frostbite."

"What's frostbite?" Exercise Bike asked.

"It's when a human's skin, or part of their body like a finger, hand, or foot, actually freezes solid. I wasn't in the room when the doctors worked on her, but I heard someone say later that she was lucky she only lost the tip of that finger. I guess they have to be really careful when they thaw out something like that. Ever see meat in a freezer?"

A few things nodded.

"It's kind of like that. Only the meat in a freezer is already dead. A living thing that gets frozen can end up dead if they don't thaw out the frozen part just right. Apparently, it's like having a little part of the person dead, and it will rot and cause lots of other problems. So they had to cut off part of that finger that they couldn't save. My owner had a lot of trouble moving her fingers after that. She had to have a lot of physical therapy. I was never around for that—just sitting on her shelf at home, waiting, but I heard her talk about it to friends on the phone. It was several months before we went out on another assignment."

Exercise Bike couldn't help making another comment. "I never realized it, but it seems we are tougher than our owners in some ways!"

"Yes, we are," 35MM said. "It was really easy to replace my lens cap. We're tough in other ways, too. My owner was anxious for a long time after that. She stuck to some pretty simple assignments—interviewing scientists in their labs and offices and such—while she got back her courage to get out into the wilderness again. When she finally did, it was to a desert area, photographing insects and spiders. She completely covered herself for protection from the sun and carried a lot of bottles of water."

"Did anyone else ever get the polar bear shot?" Gun asked.

"I'm not sure, but one time I heard her talking on the phone to someone about that location. I heard something about setting up a remote control camera that would be activated by movement so the photographer didn't have to stay out exposed to that severe cold.

"Anyway, our adventures were much fewer and not as exciting from then on. What really did me in, though, was the development of digital cameras! Faster, sharper, no more changing rolls of film, no more developing...photographers knew right away if a shot was good or not. I became obsolete. I was so jealous of her new camera that I wouldn't speak to him for the longest time.

"But my owner often picked me up in an affectionate way. I had become a keepsake. She'd take me down and show me off to friends when they came to visit. 'My first professional camera,' she'd say with pride in her voice. She would show some of the shots I'd taken, awards she'd received, and then back on the shelf I'd go to gather dust. I finally did become friends with the new camera and sometimes didn't even mind hearing about the adventures he had out on assignment—but those stories never were as good as the times I had. She did most of her work with him on rare plants and flowers in high altitude places. He got to see some of the writing she did on how changing temperatures were affecting plants. Seems like some plants are 'moving up' in altitude as lower places get too hot for them. But plants can't migrate like animals do, so there was a big concern about some of those plants surviving.

"Pretty soon we both sat on the shelf because a newer, better model camera came out! My owner wasn't as sentimental about my first replacement—gave him to her niece."

A long sigh escaped from 35MM. Everyone let the silence settle.

"One day, she wasn't sentimental about me anymore either. And here I am. Not an antique, not new, just an old camera, useless to this digital generation! One of so many things people just use up and then leave behind. I'm hoping some young photographer will buy me for their own first camera—hopefully someone who still wants to develop their own prints. That's getting to be a lost art, too."

Several items nodded in agreement. No words were needed. They knew exactly how 35MM Camera felt.

Chapter 9

Rage on the Golf Course

You have to realize that the days were busy, too, even though items did not move or talk once the shop opened each day. Customers came and went—some buying items, some selling or borrowing money based on the value of some item. Those folks always sighed as they left the shop, hoping that they could scrounge up the money to redeem their possessions before thirty days went by—after which that item could be sold and maybe wouldn't be there if the owner did return.

Plenty of untold stories went out the shop door, never to be heard by the rest of us. But that's life. People and objects come and go; nothing ever stays the same. There were nights, I'm sorry to say, that I didn't even pay attention to the stories because they were just everyday hum-drum. I can't help but record everything, but I don't have to bore you with that kind of stuff.

I perked up the night Golf Bag spoke up.

**

"Some men are such egomaniacs," he began. "This fellow who owned me fancied himself good enough to become a professional golfer. Couldn't play worth a damn, but he thought he could. Spent more time on the golf course—and a ton of money, too—than he did with his wife and kids. Have to admit I liked being used all the time, but there were weekends I wouldn't have minded a day of rest in the garage."

"Did he enter a lot of tournaments?" a first-generation iPad—who apparently had done a lot of internet searching on golf and other sports—beeped in.

"Oh, yes. Once he got lucky and got into the finals. I say lucky, because his scores were never that great, but in that round someone had dropped out due to illness and that got him into the final round. But it also blew up his ego like the Hindenburg blimp! He went home and told his wife he was going to quit his job and golf full time."

"Bet his wife liked that idea," a tool set said, following the statement with, "hardy-har-har-har."

Laughter rang through the shop. It took a few minutes for the haws and guffaws to slow down enough for Golf Bag to continue.

"Duh," Golf Bag said. "Everybody in the garage could hear that argument. That lady was ready to pack up her stuff and the kids and leave! But I guess she figured he had to get it out of his system. She agreed that he could drop to 'part time' for two months, if his boss said it was okay. If he hadn't won a substantial amount of money by that time—enough to make up for the lost pay—he'd go back to work and forget the whole pro thing."

Some of the tools covered their mouths but continued to snicker.

"Well, he sure gave it his best shot! He practiced all day two days a week—drives, putts, wedging out of sand traps… and, really, he did improve his game some. Actually took 4th in a small tournament about a month later—presenting his wife with a whopping $500.00 prize check. Which she put directly into her purse."

Another round of laughter reverberated around the shop. It was easy to see Golf Bag was enjoying the attention.

"Halfway through the second month, he entered a bigger tournament. I think he knew this was the do-or-die event. His boss and his wife were both on his case—the boss threatening to replace him and his wife threatening to leave him. The first half of the tournament he got par on every hole—his personal best! Then—and I don't know if it was the stress or his general lack of real talent—but things began to fall apart. He bogeyed three times—which dropped him out of the rankings—then landed his ball in a water trap. His head dropped to his chest. His caddy and I could hear muttered cuss words—'Sh—,effin'—, d—, *&#!' and worse. He really did turn out to be like the Hindenburg—crashed and burned!

"Then he picked up his head, took his penalty shot and tried to finish with some grain of dignity."

All items stood in a moment of respectful silence, in spite of all the earlier laughter. Some apparently knew those feelings.

Golf Bag continued. "Then on the last hole, he tried a long putt. I held my breath hoping he could just gain that one stroke and save his pride. But…no…it curved around the hole and rolled away. Even the audience groaned in sympathy. My owner bent his putter over his knee, threw that club into the water trap, where his ball already lay, and walked off the course."

Another moment of silence.

"You notice I am short a putter. You know, my owner's wife actually gave him a hug of sympathy when he got home! He crawled back to his boss, said he'd never leave him shorthanded again. Next day…well, here I am. I guess the family got back to normal—whatever that is."

"Well," Vase said, "at least his wife mended his bruised ego, and, as you say, he got it out of his system."

**

Nobody else knew quite what to say, or whether to laugh or cry. Sometimes life is just like that—people and things got to eat a little crow once in a while and carry on. People need to realize when to work harder to succeed and when they should put their passion into something else.

ChaptER 10

NEWS of TEapot

The next morning, a Monday, was on the slow side. Only one customer came in—an older man who looked at, but didn't buy, Gun. So Mr. Garcia sat behind the counter reading the news. The phone rang, so he put down the paper—leaving it opened to page two of the "City & State" section. At the bottom in the "Around the City/ State" box, among short reports on car accidents and a minor fire was a headline, "Man Arrested in Brutal Assault." As I rotated and began to scan it, I noticed that all the items closest to it were also eyeing it as best they could in their day-time frozen states. Unfortunately for me, the print was too small from my distance to make out the words.

It was definitely about Teapot's owner. As you can imagine, it was a long day for everybody waiting to be able to talk about it. The few who could see it—Vase, a stand-up collectible china Plate, and a silver Pitcher— could hardly wait to spill the news. Jewelry items and 35MM Camera below the glass counter top were not able to see it. Neither could any of the larger items like Golf Bag and Exercise Bike because they were too far away. Gun could have seen it, but he had been set down facing the wrong way after being examined by the one earlier customer and, of course, couldn't change his position during the day.

**

What a hubbub when the clock finally chimed!

"It was about her, wasn't it?"

"What did it say? What did it say?"

"Couldn't get it all ..."

**

There was so much noise and confusion, I couldn't get it all straight.

**

Once **again**, Gun shouted above the din. "Slow down, everybody. Talk one at a time!"

Vase had had the best view, so she spoke first. "The headline was 'Man Arrested in Brutal Assault.' A man in his late twenties was picked up for an assault of a young woman, also in her late twenties, at the Casa Villa apartments. That's only a few blocks from here, isn't it?"

"Yes, it's right across the street from Crystal Shores where I first lived," Exercise Bike said.

"For crying out loud!" Gun shouted. "He never left—just changed to a different apartment! Talk about stupid."

The jumble of voices began again until Plate called above the din, "Let us finish telling you!"

Several items mumbled "sorry" and things quieted down again.

"It said that the man admitted to the assault during questioning. He was booked and jailed. That's all I was able to see."

Vase continued, "Then it said that a public defender has been assigned to him. Doesn't that mean he's without funds, so he probably can't make bail either, Gun?"

"Yes, if they offered bail. I don't think they do when someone admits guilt," Gun replied and then stayed silent so Vase could continue.

"That was all I could see," she concluded.

Gun addressed Pitcher. "Did you get anything more?"

All eyes were on Pitcher now. "I read the bottom first, because that was what I could see best," she said. "The young woman, obviously Teapot's owner, was said to be out of the coma but is still in critical condition. Apparently, photos of the man and several others will be shown to her in the hospital."

All seemed to be relieved to hear that the man had been caught and that Teapot's owner was getting better.

"What does Mr. Garcia do with the newspapers after he reads them? We should watch for more about her," Vase said.

"There's a stack in the back in a plastic recycling bin— back where we play cards," a set of pliers from a tool box who had never spoken before (except during the card games and then only to say, "raise you," "call," or "I'm out") told them. "I'll be happy to take on the job of checking each day's paper if you like. I can get a grip on the corners, so it's easy for me to turn pages."

"Please, do." And, "Yeah, that'd be great," and other echoes of assent went around the room.

It was silent again until Vase said, "I don't think I know you very well, Pliers. How did you and the rest of your set come to be with us? Would you mind sharing your tale?"

"Oh, not much to tell, really," Pliers said, "but okay. We—all the box of us tools—belong to a handyman. He was getting really steady work for years. Made a good living using us to fix all kinds of things. He would fix appliances, install simple wiring for people, sometimes repair the rotting wood on a porch, stuff like that. Then his wife became ill and the hospital bills piled up. He wasn't making enough as an independent. He mumbled a lot about no insurance because it was too expensive for a self-employed person. He took a job for some big company that sells appliances that so he could get medical benefits. I remember him saying that he'd rather work for himself, but you gotta' do what you gotta' do. I'm hopeful though. He didn't sell us outright—just took out a loan—and he's been in regularly to make payments. Every time he comes in I hear him talk about working for himself again because he can qualify for some new insurance program. I also heard him tell Mr. Garcia that his wife is better now."

"Is he that older gentleman who comes in every Friday?" Gun asked.

"Yup, that's him. I don't know how much he still owes, but I'm hopeful we'll be back with him soon, working again. That's why there's no price tag on the box and we've always been in the back room."

"How nice to have an uplifting story," Plate commented. "Thank you for sharing it."

**

Most of the items had such pathetic stories that it was a great change of pace for the shop—news of Teapot and a hopeful story.

The following day, Officer Daniels came in to get a little more information from our owner.

**

"Morning, Mr. Garcia. Thought you'd like to hear the scuttlebutt around the station about your break-in. You'll never believe what that nut case is saying!"

"Oh? Would love to hear."

"Seems his lawyer is trying to claim an insanity defense."

"Didn't seem crazy when he wanted to buy that record from me."

"I wasn't around that night, but the arresting officers said he was going on and on about how a bunch of things 'jumped on him'—can you believe it?"

Mr. Garcia shook his head. "Well, if they can establish that, he must be nuts, hey? Or was he high on something?"

"I heard they did a breath test for alcohol on the spot. I'm sure they've got the results but whoever knows what's up with that, they aren't talking about it. I did hear that they drew blood when they got him back to the station."

"Thanks for the news. Maybe I'll call the detective in charge and see what he can tell me."

"Yeah, do that. They'll probably tell you, since it was your place he broke into."

**

I don't know if the others were thinking about what Officer Daniels said, but it was on my mind. What if the guy wasn't drunk or high on something? Would any humans believe what he said? Or would they go with the insanity defense?

ChaptER 11

PlatE and PitchER ShaRE TheiR LivES

*If Mr. Garcia called for information that day, it wasn't
while he was in the shop. Several items did have the
same thought I had, but after some discussion, everyone
agreed that there wasn't much they could do about it
either way. So everything settled down for another story.*

*Plate and Pitcher, who had arrived together the
week before Teapot, agreed to tell their story. Plate
was one of those "collectable" types of china plates
you sometimes see advertised on TV. He was decorated
with gold leaf edging and a gold leaf version of a
famous painting of George Washington in the middle.
Pitcher was a shapely silver-plated thing about a foot
tall. Looked like she could hold a couple of quarts of
anything.*

**

Plate began the tale. "We were both wedding gifts to what we
thought was a lovely young couple a bit over two years ago."

"It was so dreamy to think we'd be with them for many
years, maybe begin a family legacy," Pitcher added.

65

"Hum, anyway," Plate continued, "the honeymoon didn't last long. We were all still sitting in our boxes on the floor of an apartment—no, not Crystal Shores or that other place that's been mentioned—can't remember the name of it, but it was way across town. The woman, she'd snipe at him and he'd snipe right back."

"Then one day we heard, 'Remember this was only a business arrangement anyway so you could get your permanent residency!' Seems it was an 'arranged' marriage so the guy could get legal immigrant status. Apparently, they'd both put on quite a show of being very in love for everybody involved—her friends and family, the INS people…His family was thrilled for him. Her parents had put on quite an affair from what we heard. We couldn't see anything at the reception, being all wrapped up, but the conversation, music, so many voices…We saw her spend a lot of days writing little notes thanking various people for all the gifts the first few weeks.

"The man often told his business-arrangement wife to settle down, that they had to make it look good for at least a year," Pitcher added, "because INS might check up on them. 'Yeah, like they have time with all the slew of paperwork and other people they have to process,' she'd said. Then he'd say something about wasn't there some custom that wedding gifts had to be returned if a marriage broke up right away. She said that was only if the marriage lasted less than a year and they had to stick it out at least a year, so the gifts didn't need to be returned. 'But, seriously,' she said, 'what are we going to do with all this stuff?' He told her she could have it all because gifts were usually for the bride anyway."

"What is wrong with young people today?" Guitar said in a voice that sounded like a rhythm and blues song. "They get involved with all the wrong people and marry for the stupidest reasons!" He had never come down from his hooks on the wall and rarely spoke up. Some of the newer items had never heard his voice.

"Nice of you to join in, Guitar," Vase said. "But let them finish the story. Comment afterwards, please."

It was silent a minute and then Pitcher continued. "The apartment had two bedrooms, so they took to sleeping separately. They worked different hours and days—I think she was a nurse or something because she was gone twelve hours at a time and often at night, but she had more days off. They avoided each other when they were home at the same time—like roommates who don't get along but have to finish the lease. All of us gifts continued to sit in our boxes, day after day, month after month."

"Well, not quite everybody," Plate said. "They used the dishes, pots and pans, towels, sheets, etc. Those of us of a decorative nature were the ones who sat in boxes, pushed to the walls and placed behind the couch, in the walk-in closet, etc."

"Somehow, Plate and I ended up next to each other behind the recliner. Pretty dull most of the time. We could only hear the TV and couldn't see anything but the wall and the back of the easy chair. So, to avoid boredom when no one was home, we began to talk about everything and anything.'

"Mostly discussing what we heard on the various TV shows," Plate put in. "We found ourselves agreeing on most things and have become quite attached to each other in friendship."

"Our relationship has become much deeper than theirs ever was," Pitcher said, smiling at Plate. "Anyway, a year and a month after the wedding, he moved out. Some of her friends and family came to visit, consoling her about the divorce and all, suggesting maybe the difference in culture was more of an issue than they thought it would be, asking what they could do to help. She'd just assure them she was fine and would carry on. They bought into her act just as they had before. I don't think anybody else ever knew the truth about their sham of a marriage."

Plate picked up the story again. "Then one day, she began sorting all the gifts into piles and packing up everything. She muttered a lot about not needing such a large apartment and maybe going back to her hometown. We heard her on the phone talking to some hospital and her voice perked up. She said she'd send in her application right away. We spent many nights wondering what would become of us and how Pitcher and I would feel if we were separated."

"Yes," Pitcher said, winding her curved handle around Plate, "turns out we were much more compatible than they ever were. We became much more than friends. She finally moved us out from behind the chair and looked at us with the most disgusting look. I couldn't blame her concerning me. I felt so ashamed. I'd grown quite tarnished over the many months. 'I absolutely *hate* the idea of having to polish silver, and why would anybody think I'd want to collect President Plates? These definitely go in the sell pile,' the woman said."

"But, Pitcher, you know how I feel about you," Plate said. "I had to dry a lot of tears that night," he added to the rest of the items.

"Yes, knowing how much we cared for each other had made life bearable. Now we had to worry about being separated. A week or so later, she loaded us and several other decorative items into her car. She stopped at several different pawn shops, taking a few things at a time, spreading it around so she'd get more money. Each time she grabbed a box, we were afraid we'd be ripped apart, but here we are, still together!" Plate said.

**

68

No one wanted to say, although they surely all felt it because I could see it in their eyes, that the likelihood of the two of them being sold to the same customer was slim to none. Maybe we all wanted to believe their "marriage" would not end the way their owners had. We all have to hope in something.

The next day was Friday and Tool Box's owner made the final payment on his loan. Pliers gave us a smile as he and the rest of the tool set were carried out the door. Now who would scan the newspaper every day for news of Tea Pot?

Chapter 12

Guitar Sings His Life

As I mentioned earlier, Guitar had never come down from his hooks on the wall and rarely spoke. But the night after Tool Box left us, he offered to tell, or I should say sing, his story. His rich tenor voice strummed away in a concert of sorts, beginning with a lively '50s rock-and-roll beat.

**

"Oh, I'm one for the money
    Two for the show,
    Three to get ready
    Now, go man, go," he began.

"Oh, a lot of people have played tunes on me. The most famous was my first—Elvis Presley."

Gun was immediately critical. "Oh, come on, if you'd belonged to The King you wouldn't be here! You'd be in the Rock and Roll Hall of Fame or at his place in Memphis, or some other place like that."

Everybody glared at Gun. It was extremely rude to interrupt any item's story and insult them to boot.

71

"Hey," Guitar strummed, "nobody questioned Teapot over her brush with historical fame. She and I have a similar problem—we know who owned us and used us, but have no paperwork to prove it. Yes, it takes away from our dollar value, but WE know who we are!"

"Sorry," Gun muttered, properly chastened.

"I have to admit, I wasn't much impressed with Elvis when he first began to play on me. I grinned and groaned out a lot of bad cords, but every beginner is that way. His voice was NEVER that of a beginner and gradually he got better at playing me. I won't bore you with the details of his rise to fame and all that—anyone can find that on the internet and in books. Gun, I'll also admit that I was never the instrument he played on stage. I was the backstage, background guy used to practice and create.

"Once he made the Big Time, I was used less and less. Then one night after a performance, an assistant stage hand left me behind. Sadly, I don't think I was even missed because nobody ever came back inquiring about me. I sat, out of tune and covered with dust in a corner of that theater for many months."

At this point, Guitar's song changed from the lively rock-and-roll beat to a slow blues style that a depressed jazz player might use.

"And I was sooooo looooonnnnnely Iiiiiiiiiiiiiiiiiiiiiii could cryyyyyyyyy ..."

There wasn't an item in the shop that didn't know THAT feeling.

"I don't know quite how long I sat there," Guitar continued, "but finally one night, a new stage hand spotted me. She asked around as to my owner, but nobody knew, so the theater manager told her she could have me. Now this young woman wanted so much to play me. She talked to everyone she knew about her aspirations as a singer. She even hired someone to teach her to play—not easy on a stage hand's pay. She practiced and practiced, tried and tried, but, now that I think about it, she was a bit like Golf Bag's owner—all the desire but not a speck of talent. Poor thing got booed off several low-life bar stages. Also, like Golf Bag's owner, she finally wised up. I ended up in a pawn shop for the first time—there have been others. Have to say, this place has been the nicest."

A round of smiles and "yeah, yeahs" went through the shop.

"After a short time at that first shop—believe it was in Memphis—I was bought by another aspiring youngster. This young woman, while she never became a house-hold name, did quite well for herself." The tune now changed to the twang of Country Western love songs. "She traveled all over the country in a beat-up old car playing for tips in honkey-tonks. We had some grand times—just me and her and the pickle jar for tips, on a tiny stage. So small she didn't need a mic. Went from Montana to Texas and from LA to the Jersey shore.

"Now and again, she hooked up with some guy or other, but those flings never lasted. She'd just grab her stuff and take off again. I do think those were my best years. But we all know nothing lasts forever. Train whistles blew, called to her. Wouldn't you know? She finally got tired of drifting and found a guy—an engineer on a train—would you believe it? She settled down with him, raised a bunch of kids. Put me in the attic where only an occasional mouse strummed my strings while running across me."

Now the song was a mix of blues and more modern country.

"She and her husband were cleaning the attic years later and she found me again. 'Huh!' she said, 'here's my old guitar!'

Her husband remarked that their youngest son was about the right age to play. So she polished up my wood, restrung me and started teaching him. Even though I had to go back to those sour chords of all beginners, it WAS good to be played again.

"But that kid didn't have it—the desire, I mean. 'You're like your dad,' she said one day. 'If you want to quit, it's okay by me.' He looked at the floor and said, 'Sorry, Mom. But thanks, 'cause I just really don't like it.' So, I ended up in another pawn shop—this time in West Texas."

Guitar paused for a minute. No one spoke.

"You aren't bored, are you?" Guitar asked.

"No, no," everyone said. "We're enjoying your life's song."

"Well, the rest is a lot more of the same. There was one young man who played quite well. He led his tiny church congregation in lovely hymns. Then he got a higher calling and entered a seminary. He had no time left to play, so once again, another pawn shop. Where was that? Oh, yes, East Texas Piney Woods area. I've gone from one teenager to the next, some with talent but no desire. Others with desire but no talent. Nobody ever realizes that to make it big, it takes a LOT of BOTH. So many young people think the music world is a fast trip to fame and fortune. I think that's true of any of the creative arts; visual art, like Vase's maker, those who paint, those who aspire to write—they all have to have a lot of perseverance. Sports stars, too. Work and dedication, and practice, practice, practice."

He cast a knowing glance at Golf Bag. "Since I am only an acoustic guitar and all serious modern musicians want the new electric versions that huge stages and modern audiences require, I doubt if I'll ever see a stage again.

"But you know what? I'm not sorry about any of it. I know before long, I'll be in the hands of another kid who wants to learn. It's actually a good feeling to be the instrument that starts them off. Who knows? Maybe the next one to learn will have everything it takes and make the Big Time. And I'll have the satisfaction of knowing I gave them their start. Just like with Elvis. Even if the rest of the world never knows it or appreciates me, I've been in the heart of lots of kids and it's a good place to be."

** **

There was no need for an encore. All the items provided a quiet standing ovation and then returned to their day places to enjoy the memory of a lovely concert and the story of a guitar who truly knew how to live.

Chapter 13

More News of Teapot's Owner

I've seen things come and go from this shop for a long time. There are two basic reasons people bring things into a pawn shop. One is that they just want to get rid of something which might have some value. These people sell the item outright and usually get somewhere around half the value of the item, because the pawn shop owner has to make a profit to stay in business, of course. The second way is when someone desperate for money takes out a loan using the item as collateral. These people hope to come back and get that item when their financial situation improves—like the handyman. They, of course, pay interest on the loan—an amount that varies by shop, but usually as set amount per month. I know all this from hearing it explained a million times to people who come in with items to sell or pawn.

Either way, a new item is not put up for sale immediately. Sometimes the owner of the item wants an expert appraisal to get the best price for that object. Other times, Mr. Garcia, or any other pawn shop owner, wants an appraisal so he can set the highest price for sale. Also, many shops have a twenty-one-day waiting period to see if police drop by for a "stolen" item. Once an item is officially for sale, there is a wide range of time where it might sit on the shelves here. Some Zippo Lighters once sold the same day they became available. We might see others here, like figurines and decorative pieces, for a year or more. Overheard phone conversations between Mr. Garcia and other pawn shop owners have taught me that what sells quickly or slowly varies greatly from one neighborhood to another.

On occasion, owners will sell or trade items with each other to see if they will sell more quickly somewhere else. Mr. Garcia is the type of owner who will sometimes tell a person, "I don't have a big market here for your 'something-or-other', but you might get a good price for this from 'so-and-so on such-and-such street'." A couple of times, a person came here to sell something because another shop owner recommended our location.

It's a happy day when a man like the handyman with the tool set makes a final payment and takes his stuff back. It's a sad day when someone who borrowed against an item comes to retrieve it and it's been sold.

I hope you didn't find that explanation boring, but some people just don't know.

The day after Guitar's story was one of those sad days.

**

The bell on the door jangled and a young black man came in. The bell brought Mr. Garcia out from the back room. "May I help you?"

"Yes, I'm here to pay off my mother's loan on an antique gold necklace."

"What's the name?"

"Sylvia Smith—common name, I know, but I have the ticket here," the young man said, reaching into his pocket.

"This is over a year old," Mr. Garcia said as he typed the name into his computer. "Ah, here it is. It seems your mother made a couple payments, extended the loan twice, and then we didn't hear from her again. I'm sorry, but the necklace sold several months ago."

** **

That sale was before the items had begun to tell their stories each night. It would be hard to check back now to see what that necklace even looked like because my tapes get replaced every couple of weeks. Then the tapes stay in the back room a few months, just in case they are needed, and if they aren't called for, then I record something new over what was there.

** **

The young man's head dropped forward slightly and he sighed. "Why didn't someone call her to say she needed to come in?"

"I'm really sorry, but I can't always be calling when every loan is due. It's up to people to keep track of that themselves. I even have an extra month 'grace period' that I observe—many shops don't—but that was up long ago, too. Shows here," he turned the computer screen around, "we did try to call but the number was disconnected. Once a piece of jewelry goes into the case, it sells pretty quickly and I think I remember that was a particularly pretty piece."

The young man sighed again. "Yeah, and an heirloom, too. Mom didn't admit to borrowing against it for a while. Our family's been through some rough times. Once my mom did tell us, I guess I knew, deep down, that coming in here was a long shot, but I had to try. I was just hoping maybe it hadn't sold yet."

Mr. Garcia shrugged his shoulders. "I'm sorry, too, but there's nothing I can do."

The young man's shoulders sagged as he turned and walked out the door.

**

I felt sorry for him, kind of wishing we'd heard that story before the jewelry item sold. I was hoping some of the items would remember it and talk about it later that night. It was quiet for a while, so Mr. Garcia started skimming through the newspaper. Several pairs of eyes turned to see what they could—we all missed Plier's daily scan of the paper in the back room. Nobody else had stepped up to take over—most of them weren't equipped to be able to turn newspaper pages easily.

**

Just then, in walked Officer Daniels. Everyone was instantly alert. Like the last time we'd seen him, he had a file in his hand and pulled out a photo of a gold college class ring. "Don't suppose you've seen this?"

Mr. Garcia looked carefully but shook his head. "The last class ring I had in here was at least a year ago—they don't sell well cause nobody wants someone else's ring that's been personalized like this." He pointed out the year and initials in the photo.

"Had to try."

Then Mr. Garcia asked the question everything was waiting for. "Hey, just curious, any news on that assault case? I always skim the city briefs, but haven't seen much lately."

"Last I heard, there was going to be some kind of plea bargain. Oh, yeah, and the young woman definitely identified the guy. Guess she got released from the hospital. That's all I know. You aren't likely to see anything else in the paper since that case is sort of wrapped up and it's not a major case, so to speak."

"Thanks. I keep thinking about her. Let me know if you hear anything."

"I'll try. Been pretty busy lately. Can't get in here much except on official business. Hey, here's my card. I'll put my email on the back." He pulled a pen from his pocket and jotted it down. "This is my home email, so it's okay to do 'non official' communication on it."

"Great. Here's one of my cards, too—email's right on there." Garcia picked up a card from a little holder full of cards on the counter and handed it to Officer Daniels. "Oh, and the guy who broke in here plea-bargained, too. I had to admit, even when he came in here, he seemed a little bit 'off' if you know what I mean. He didn't get away with anything here and the only real damage was the back door, which my insurance covered. Anyhow, he pled guilty to a lesser charge of breaking and entering and the DA agreed to get him into a mental health program. I was okay with that."

**

That night all the items buzzed with discussion about Tea Pot, so they never did talk about that piece of jewelry from earlier in the day, and I didn't ask, so I guess I'll never know. All were glad to hear her owner had recovered and that her lousy boyfriend wouldn't be free any time soon—or so everyone hoped. Once that talk ended, a fairly new TV spoke up.

**

"Anybody want to listen to where I've been?"

"Sure, sure," echoed around the room.

"It's not as exciting as some of your tales and not long because I'm fairly new, but maybe you'll like it."

35MM Camera reassured TV. "Go ahead. We are not a group to judge anybody here—or most of us at least try not to be judgmental." He gave Gun a quick glance as he said that.

"Okay, then, here goes. It's kind of exciting to be unpacked and placed out on display in the electronics section of a big store. There's so much to see every day as people come in, look around, and buy something. I don't remember anyone ever talking like we do here, though. This is a very special place. I also remember hoping as each person glanced at me that they would buy me. All of us so want to be owned and used."

"Yes, yes," several things agreed.

"I'm not the biggest, or the fanciest model out there, so my price was reasonable enough for just about anybody to afford me, especially when the store knocked off a couple hundred for a Labor Day Weekend sale. The store was really busy all weekend. I watched several TVs like me, some computers, DVD players and tons of stuff get carried out the door before a young woman with two kids in tow looked at me and read my tag. She said, 'Hmmm,' and, 'Umm,' to herself a bunch of times before a salesperson finally asked if she could help her.

"The young woman shushed her two little boys and then said, 'Yes, does this TV have a way to block out some channels on cable? I don't want my kids flipping the remote and seeing, well, you know …'

"The sales person replied, 'Oh, I know exactly what you mean. I have kids, too. Yes, there's a way in the remote—I'll show you if you like—to do that.'

"Then the young woman asked about financing—seems she didn't have much money and not much credit. 'But I just got a new job,' she said.

"The sales person said that wouldn't be a problem—all their customers needed to do was provide an employer's phone number, address and a boss' name. So, they walked to the counter and I watched as the young woman filled out all the paperwork—the two boys were pulling at her, all excited to get their new TV home. That finally got finished up. Then the sales person found out that I was the last of that particular model in stock. 'Are you willing to accept a floor model? There's actually an extra discount for that.'

"The young woman was thrilled! A stock room person brought out the box I'd been shipped to the store in and they packed me up—not quite as well as I'd first been packaged, but safely enough. The stock room person carried me out to the young woman's beat up, older-model Chevy Cobalt (I notice things like that) and loaded me in the trunk. I just fit. Those boys were bouncing all over the place saying, 'Yea! Yea! Can we watch Sponge Bob when we get home?' Their mother told them she had to set me up first.

"So I arrived at my new home—a small but neat apartment—the converted garage of an old house. Later I learned that the house belonged to the young woman's mother. The young woman told her kids about how her grandmother—their great-grandmother—had once lived here in the garage-apartment. Her mother—the kids' grandma—had taken care of her. She told her kids some of the good memories she had from her childhood and sitting with Granny. Now she was the one who needed a place to raise her kids. 'Your dad tried, but…,' she said. Apparently, the kids' dad had run off and left them with nothing.

"The young woman—whose name I never did catch more than 'Mom' or 'Honey'—followed the directions the store clerk gave her, programing the remote to block certain channels, and got me all hooked up to a cable outlet and soon I was showing Sponge Bob to a couple supper happy little boys.

"Those were lovely days. Grandma babysat the boys while the young mother worked. Sometimes they were over in her house and sometimes in the garage apartment. Grandma didn't just let the kids watch the Cartoon Network all day. I went back and forth between that, the Disney Channel, an educational station, and some daytime drama when the boys had their naps. It was everything all of us dream about.

"Fortunately for that little family, unfortunately for me, their lives got better and better. I think it was two years later that the young woman got a promotion at work. She was now earning enough to afford a bigger place. The two boys started school and didn't stay with Grandma anymore—I heard talk about an after-school program and how Grandma needed a rest sometimes. Along with the bigger place to live, came a bigger TV, and, well, here I am. I just hope another family buys me soon."

"Don't we all?" said a newly-acquired lap top who was still on the not-for-sale shelf.

Gun looked around at everyone and mumbled, "Not me. I never want to see a family again."

**

I wondered what he meant by that, but you know I choose not to talk or ask questions. I just record. I can actually do my job better when no one realizes what I'm doing up here.

Chapter 14

Antique Clock Chimes More Than Midnight

The next night, we heard Antique Clock's voice in his chime. "If. You. Don't. Mind. May. I. Tell. My. Sto-. Ry. To-. Night?" While he chimed each word, I wondered if we would have to listen to the whole thing that way, but once his deep bass bonging ended, his voice was more "regular".

Several nods let Clock know to proceed.

**

"I don't go back as far as Teapot did, but pretty close. I was built in the 1830s and I have to say I'm proud that I was the latest technology in smaller 'Grandfather' type clocks for my day. I only need to be wound every thirty hours, not twenty-four, so I can be wound up at the same time each day before I've stopped. If an owner forgets for a few hours, I keep right on ticking.

"I had several owners early on—none of them particularly memorable—and I wasn't a 'family heirloom' until, oh, I don't know, maybe the fourth or fifth owner. Somewhere in the late 1860s, my owner at the time—a lady—decided she had to do something about the fact that my tick-tock is fairly quiet and

87

she had a hard time seeing my pendulum swing back and forth. So, she dug around in a small metal box and pulled out a lapel button with an image of Abraham Lincoln on it—and it was an authentic Lincoln campaign button, but back then, people didn't seem to think such a thing had any value. Watching the button cross back and forth through a little circle in the floral decorations painted on my 'door' told her instantly from a distance if I was running or not. She also decided to paint the wooden columns on my sides with a gold-leaf paint to 'dress me up' she said.

"I thought I might become a legacy in that family, but many years later, her only son decided he didn't want me. When he went to sell me, he found out that the coat of paint had destroyed whatever 'antique value' I might one day have. 'Oh,' he groaned, 'My mother never thought anything about things like that,' and sold me for a piddling amount. I don't know why, but neither that man nor the shop owner purchasing me noticed the Lincoln campaign button that remained on my pendulum. Honestly, it was worth more than I was by that time!"

**

I'm sure a few items wondered where that Lincoln button was—since there was NOTHING on his pendulum now. However, everyone remained quiet and allowed Clock to continue.

**

"I was rather a fixture in that shop—just sitting there, never wound, never speaking, just watching things in the store come and go. Years and years went by. I began to wonder if I would ever be owned again, if anyone would ever wind me up. Then one day a man and his wife came into the store. They looked around at several items and then the woman's eyes landed right on me. I think that was sometime in the 1930s, but there was never a calendar in the shop to know for sure.

"She walked over to me and said, 'Chester, wouldn't this clock be just perfect on the mantle at our summer home on the lake?'

"The man came over. 'I believe you are right, Jessie. Let's buy it.' And so they did. A very long drive over mostly gravel roads later, I was carried in and placed on the most unique mantle I've ever sat on! It was a quarter of a birch log—with the bark still on it—fixed to a huge stone fireplace in a beautiful house built entirely of logs! The room was huge—dining and living combined—with one-foot-square beams supporting what I assumed was a second story. I tick-tocked and chimed my way through many happy summers, but when the snow flew late each fall, the house would be closed up 'for the season'. Then I was alone and quiet with the furniture, the pictures on the walls, and a few mice that moved into various corners every winter to get out of the snow in the meadows round about.

"Occasionally, I was unable to start up when they came back in the late spring, so off I would go to a clock repairman who would take me apart, clean all my gears and works, and put me back in running order. I always ticked more joyfully after that, and I noticed that my sound reverberated through the mantle to the stone, to the wood in the surrounding logs louder than ever—a peaceful sound the people said on more than one occasion.

"Now Chester and Jessie had a daughter, Celia—their only child—who grew into a lovely young woman. There was this particular young man who called on her quite often—over a number of years, since Celia was still pretty young—just fourteen—when they first met. Didn't take long for those two long to fall in love."

Several sighs floated around the shop.

"I heard they married over one winter and then left the area—the man, Clarke, was an army officer and World War II had just broken out. By the time they returned home after the war, they already had a boy and a girl. They began to spend a lot of days during the summer—mostly on the weekends—at the log house, which they had begun to call 'The Cabin.' It was such fun to watch those little ones play on the floor beneath me. Another baby girl arrived and then after a space of a few years, but in quick succession to each other, two more, also girls, came along. One fall, Chester must have passed away, because he never came back after the summer the last girl was born. Jessie stopped staying there all the time—maybe she didn't like being there without her husband—but the young couple and their five children stayed all summer every year, and often into the fall.

"Excuse me," Clock said as he bonged just once.

"Oh, those were joyous years! Surely I would be a legacy now I said to myself many times. That youngest child just loved it when her daddy lifted her up to peek inside me and turn the key round and round to wind me up. Many years later, I heard her tell one of her children that the sound of my ticking and chiming during the night—which she could hear through the wood clear upstairs—gave her a feeling of comfort if she woke in the night."

There was a brief pause in Clock's story, as if he was hesitant to continue. "Am I boring you?" he asked.

"No, no," everyone assured him.

"So many of you have said it that I hesitate to repeat it, but if you are well-built, you tend to last longer than your owners. I had ticked and chimed through a great many summers sitting on that mantle. The children grew up and left home one by one. But then they would return to visit with a new round of babies. Celia and Clarke actually did a lot of remodeling of the log home, turning it into a year-round place, much to my happiness, even though they were no longer winding me because they thought I could not be repaired. We passed many cozy winters together while the snow piled up outside. Sometimes they would leave for the worst winter months, but the day came when they grew so old they didn't want to make those trips south.

"The cycles of the seasons keep going even when humans can't. There was one lovely winter just before Christmas when all five of the 'children' came to celebrate Celia's 80th birthday. Sadly, not even two months later, they were all back, along with a whole bunch of grown grandchildren, too, and a couple of great-grandchildren…for the funeral.

"They laughed and talked, sang and shared many precious memories. But I was concerned for my future. None of the grown children or grandchildren lived anywhere close. Clarke began to make plans to sell the place. He didn't want to be there alone any more than Jessie had."

Clock couldn't help it; he signaled another break. Bong! Bong!

"The following summer, the 'girls' came back to divide up all the things Clarke didn't plan to take with him. Everything was packed in boxes. I guess I needn't have worried—that youngest daughter took me with her! I went first to a repair shop and happily ticked away once cleaned and rebalanced. The man who repaired me told my new owners that I needed to sit in a perfectly level place. I sat on a table in the summer home they had, and were fixing up, for a time and then was packed carefully into their car for a very long journey south.

"I was placed with care on top of an antique piano. Once they'd placed me on top of a couple of pieces of wood—to keep me level because the piano wasn't quite level—I was wound

91

daily again. My only problem then was that I was left behind for the summer! The youngest of their daughters was there all summer, but she didn't seem to think about winding me—ever. Whenever my child-now-woman-now-grandmother owner was gone (whether for a weekend or the summer season) I simply had to wait for her return to be wound.

"Relationships with humans come and go, some strong and lasting, others not so much. I'm sorry to say...."

"It's all right," Vase said softly. "I think we all know what came next."

It looked like Clock might stop ticking right then and there. He seemed to choke over what came next. "The worst was that someone took the Lincoln button before they...before they." But Clock couldn't finish.

**

Everyone slipped quietly away. Clock chimed out the rest of the night, but he never spoke again. I thought to myself how sad it is that humans often don't realize the need that things have to be wanted, used for their specific purposes. It is okay that they no longer want something themselves— but it's so true: one person's "trash" is indeed another person's "treasure." If only they'd think to find new owners who would care about an object. If only people would think about the object itself. I know that somethings wear out or break and need to be thrown out, but other things last and last. It would be nice if people would utilize that aspect of many objects they own.

Chapter 15

Gun Finally Opens Up

Gun sat down on his butt with a thump the next evening. Everyone had stopped asking him about himself, so nobody so much as looked at him. Instead, they glanced around at each other, especially at those who had not yet told their stories, looking to see who would speak up. Sales had been brisk of late and many items had gone out the door with not much new coming in.

**

It came as rather a surprise when Gun almost whispered, "I have a confession."

All eyes turned to him. Vase's gentle voice was just as quiet. "Gun, you've done nothing to confess about here."

Gun sighed, his barrel pointing upward—an unusual stance for him in the shop. He'd always pointed upward, or at someone, but never downward. "No, not here, not exactly… but my story is a confession, and if you'll hear me, I'm ready to tell it."

**

Everybody settled down and sat quietly. I've never been in a cathedral, but from what I've heard, a place like that would have been noisier than the shop at that moment.

**

"I never lied to anybody here," Gun began, "but I sure didn't give you any really truthful impressions of myself either."

No one spoke. Silence continued for almost a full minute.

"I did belong to an FBI agent. I didn't lie about that. But I wasn't his service weapon. I never went on one day's work with him. I was his personal weapon at home. Usually, I was locked up in a glass-door cabinet in the living room. That's where I heard bits and pieces of what he did at work, but not much because he didn't talk a lot about the cases he worked. He always said he would not bring work home with him, or that he was not allowed to discuss cases outside the office—confidentiality thing. But I watched a lot of cop shows on TV. All that bragging those nights playing in the back room was just what I got from cop shows on TV. So I'm really sorry for all that."

"No problem." "It's okay," and other such comments burbled out of various items.

Gun continued. "A time came when there were some burglaries in the neighborhood. My owner got worried about his wife and young son. So he took his wife, and me, down to a shooting range and taught her how to use me properly. He wanted her to feel safe and confident because he had gotten a promotion and there was a possibility he'd have to go out of town on some cases. That young mother didn't want to at first. She told him she didn't trust herself with a gun—was afraid she'd hesitate if she were ever faced with needing to use it. They talked gently about this several times, but she finally understood the need. She practiced with me every week, with him standing behind her, coaching her. At one point he said, 'You can shoot almost as well as I can!'

"She looked at him seriously and said, 'I hope I never have to use this thing, ever.'

"He put both arms around her. 'I hope not, too, but if you ever do, don't hesitate, shoot! In the moment you hesitate, an intruder could disarm you and use the gun on you. Do you understand?' She nodded.

"Over another few weeks, he taught her a lot of other self-defense moves, not involving me. In one practice session, she flipped him and pinned him down. They both laughed and he told her he didn't have to worry now when he had to be away.

"I returned to my place in the cabinet in the living room. Every day, I watched her and that little boy. He grew out of toddlerhood and into a little kid. The channel on their set got changed to the same kind of stuff TV told you about. Life went on, and it was good. My owner had gone out of town once or twice, but only for two or three days.

"Then a big case came up. My owner came home to pack a suitcase, telling his wife he would probably be gone a couple of weeks. 'I'll call you every evening,' he said. And he did. He would talk to their son early in the evening, and then call her back later. They'd talk, and talk, and talk. She missed him, she always said. And the noises around the house at night bothered her. He reassured her—the local police had caught that burglar, he reminded her, 'and you know where the gun is. Go to the range and practice if you want.'

"She did just that—left their boy with a friend's mom and shot off several rounds on me. When she came home, she started to put me in the locked cabinet and then mumbled to herself, 'What good will the gun do locked in here? It's in the bedroom

95

that I would need it.' So she closed the cabinet and put me in the drawer of the nightstand next to the bed. 'And I shouldn't have to search for ammo in the dark if there is an intruder,' she continued, leaving me loaded right there in the drawer."

Gun shuddered. He couldn't speak for a few minutes. It seemed everyone was starting to guess what would come next, but nobody said a word. Vase reached out to Gun, but he pulled back a bit.

"No, I have to finish!" he said.

"A couple days went by. Things were okay. It was the day before my owner was due back. They had actually solved the case more quickly than they thought they would. That morning, she was in the living room, running the vacuum. The boy came into the bedroom, looking around for the teddy bear he had dropped after climbing in bed with his mom. He looked under the bed—no bear. He looked in the closet—no bear. He looked under a pile of clothes by the night stand—no bear. He looked at the drawer. Now you need to know that I was guessing all this by the sounds in the room. The drawer was closed and I couldn't see, but my hearing is very sharp, and it wasn't the first time he had to go looking for his bear. It was, however, the first time since she had put me in the drawer.

"Light poured into the drawer. There were these round little eyes looking at me. 'Wow!' escaped his lips. He reached out for me. 'NO, NO, NO!' I yelled. 'Put me back! Don't touch me!' But of course, he couldn't hear me. He looked at me one way and another. Turned me upside down, right side up.

"Then suddenly I was looking right at his face with my barrel. I was in a panic! I couldn't even breathe. 'Please,' I said to the God they talked about on TV on Sunday mornings, and said Grace to before every meal, 'Make him put me down.'

"For a minute, he turned me around again. But then he turned me toward him again, looking straight down my barrel, like he was trying to peek down that dark tube. I was totally helpless. There was NOTHING I could do to stop him. I guess God doesn't listen to guns, only to people. I yelled anyway, 'Take your thumb off that trigger! Stop! Stop! Oh, Mom, pull the to cord off that vacuum. Get your #@&* self in here and stop him!'

"Then...then...I went off. I got hotter as the bullet spiraled down my barrel. Then I seemed to be falling and bounced on the carpet. I kept shouting, 'I'm sorry! I'm sorry! I couldn't stop him!' but the mother couldn't hear me."

**

Everyone listening began to cry—even the so-called 'manly' stuff. For a few minutes, Gun wept as much as a gun could. The items gathered around him, trying to ease his grief, and what they felt, too—a big group hug. I wished I could reach out, too, but I'm stuck up in my bracket, and, more importantly, I still didn't want to reveal that I've been recording all of this.

**

Gun took several deep breaths and then continued. "The sound of my shot brought Mom running. Her scream was so loud! She dropped to the floor and scooped up her little boy—covering herself with his blood, sobbing, screaming. It was a neighbor who heard her screaming, came barging in the front door of their house and called 911.

"An ambulance arrived. They practically had to pry the boy from the mother's arms. She rode in the ambulance. I heard later that the doctors tried everything, but couldn't save that little boy. Police arrived, too. I was picked up, processed, and then returned to my owner—out of respect for his position.

They made a report but never filed any charges. How can you punish a woman for something like that more than she would later punish herself?

"It was even worse what happened afterward. I got locked back up in the cabinet again, of course, but neither my owner nor his wife could get over their grief, or their sense of guilt. He'd give her these looks and say, 'I told you to always keep it locked up. What were you thinking?'

"And she would respond, 'I told you before—if someone did break in, what good would having a gun be if I couldn't get to it?' Round and round it went. I heard them talk about going to counseling. A lot of evenings they went off somewhere together. I assumed it was to a counselor because each time they went, they would come back a little better. But it didn't last. He blamed her; she blamed herself. The arguments got worse and worse.

"It was the mother who finally moved out. Then he did, too. A 'For Sale' sign went up in the front yard. And I ended up here. And I never want to be part of any family again." Gun's voice dropped back to a whisper, "If I could take myself apart, I would."

The others all reached out to touch Gun gently. Everyone seemed to sense that no words of theirs would help him at that moment. After several minutes, Vase said, "Gun, I think you've helped yourself the most by telling us all this. It couldn't have been easy to say after all this time. But now that you've gotten it out, faced it, you'll be able to find your way in this world again. You'll be ready for a new owner when someone does buy you."

**

They all just sat there. No one saying anything, group hugging again, until the sky began to lighten. The key turned in the back lock and everybody scurried to their places before the shop owner entered the salesroom.

Chapter 16

And Then

Nobody told any stories the following night. Nobody felt like playing games in the back room either. It was as if the magic, if it ever was that, had left and they couldn't or didn't want to talk at all again. I kept recording the silence, of course; I had to. It's my job.

Customers came and went the next day, like always. Plate got sold, leaving Pitcher behind. I saw all their faces, trying to say goodbye to Plate, wondering what Pitcher would do without him. But when night came, no one spoke, or even moved. Another day. New things came in. They didn't introduce themselves when the clock chimed. I realized how much I missed the stories and began to wish Gun had never spoken up.

A man came in, looked at Gun. He and Garcia discussed all Gun's features. Garcia told him about the requirements, the waiting period, background check, etc. required to purchase a firearm. The man filled out paperwork, took his receipt and said he would be back at the end of the waiting period. So we knew Gun would be leaving soon. When I looked at him, Gun looked more resigned to it than happy about it.

I began to think the magic had really ended, but that night they finally began to talk again.

**

"Gun," Vase said, "you are going to be all right. You have to believe that."

"Yeah, I know," he said. "I didn't mean to make the rest of you stop telling stories."

"It's okay," they all replied.

**

I suppose everybody needed to do some thinking about all of it, all of their stories, how small their troubles had seemed by comparison, how wrongly they had judged Gun. Several of them even told Gun they were sorry for what they had said at earlier times. More group hugging, but no new stories.

No one was prepared for what happened the next day.

**

First thing in the morning, a young woman entered the shop. Mr. Garcia said his usual, "What can I do for you?"

She answered, "My name is Anna Wentworth. I'm looking for a specific item and another dealer said he'd seen something like it here. It's a…Oh, my God! There it is! That vase on your top shelf!" Her hands started shaking.

That wasn't all the shaking going on. Vase looked like she could have screamed for joy but she didn't, probably remembering how that thief freaked out when things moved.

"This one?" Mr. Garcia said, reaching for Vase.

"Yes! Yes! I always hoped I'd find it, but I almost gave up. I've been searching for so long."

Every item in the shop looked toward the counter. Vase was as shocked as everybody else.

"It's certainly a beautiful piece," Mr. Garcia said, "Which is why I bought it, but …"

"I know you wouldn't know," the young woman began, "but this vase was made by my mother! See, here on the bottom—Abba—it was sold by accident after she died when I was a child."

"Abba? That 1980s singing group?"

The young woman laughed. "No, it's not for the singing group. That's what everyone else thought, too. It's for a song. It's a hymn my mother sang to me as a child, every night." Then the strains of that song Vase had sung so many nights ago, Abba, Abba Father…came sweetly from Anna's mouth. Then she told Mr. Garcia how she had decided to study art, antiques and everything related to that when she grew up. She had become a wholesale antique and art dealer traveling the country. She thought that would be the best way she might find the vase her mother had made especially for her so long ago. The room suddenly seemed lighter, brighter than it ever had before.

"Well, in that case, this vase is yours," Mr. Garcia said.

"No, you need to make a living, too. I'm happy to pay your listed price. This vase is priceless to me."

Everyone was smiling, Vase most of all, as she was carefully wrapped and boxed for safe travel.

If that wasn't enough for one day, around lunch time, another young woman came in. "Hello," she said to Mr. Garcia, "I know you don't know me, but I wanted to say thank you."

Mr. Garcia gave her a confused look.

"Let me explain," she said as she took a photo from her purse. "My name is Laura. Thanks to you, I got this back."

We could all see the photo she put on the counter. It was TEAPOT! And a couple of cups and saucers—cracks showing, but back in one piece!

She continued, "It was because of you, and your security camera footage, that my ex-boyfriend was arrested. It took a while, but they finally gave me my teapot back. I got all the pieces of broken cups and saucers back, too, but I only was able to glue a few back together. I just needed to tell you that, to say thank you."

"You are very welcome. I heard only a little about the case after Officer Daniels came and found your teapot. So how are you doing?"

"Well, I've recovered—physically at least—and I'm getting better in other ways, too. There is this women's support group for victims of family violence—they sort of adopted me. They helped me apply for subsidized housing and get a better apartment—not bigger, just better—and they've helped me get back on my feet. I've studied for and gotten my G.E.D. Soon, I'll be enrolling in community college with some grants and loans. I've got a part-time job. I've been able to get some help at a Community Mental Health Center—I still have nightmares sometimes. But this women's group—they're so great. Lots of them have been where I was. They've given me the courage I need to keep getting up every day, to keep trying to make my life stay on track. Someday, because of them, maybe I'll be able to pay it forward and reach out to somebody else like me."

"Well, that's great! Who would have thought?"

"Anyway, thank you for the part you played."

"It was nothing."

"Maybe nothing to some, but it was important to me."

**

And so it seemed that everything had worked out for good. I was really looking forward to that night's conversations.

But late in the day, a service van pulled up front. The driver entered carrying two boxes—the new-fangled type security cameras that look like gumball globes!

Oh, no! I'm being replaced! I've got to hurry before they pull my plug. Look at that. It's going to take TWO cameras to do the job I've done all these years! Will these new cameras record the stories? Will they save it all like I have? Will the things for sale still tell their stories? Will these new cameras care? What are their stories? Will people look around at the objects they own and wonder about those things' stories? What is your story? What is...blink ...

Author's note:

This novella started over coffee with another author. We had both been in a consignment shop a few days before and our conversation went, along with our imaginations, to what happens to the "detritus of our lives." Then we got into "what if ..." and what a great book the concept of things telling their stories might make. She decided not to run with it, and I did. So thanks, Cyndi, for letting me fly with "our" idea. Later, another author friend in my critique circle brought to my attention that some scientists actually have some theories about the idea that some animals and plants might indeed have a "life of their own". She provided the following web site and comments:

http://www.scientificamerican.com/article/is-consciousness-universal/

> "The explanation of Panpsychism I [my friend] liked best was by Christian de Quincey. He said, 'If both mind and matter are real, and are not separate substances, and neither can emerge or evolve from the other, then both matter and mind have always existed together, are coextensive, co-eternal and in some way, co-creative. Panpsychism, variously called panexperientalism or radical materialism,

proposes that matter (or physical energy) itself is intrinsically sentient or experiential, all the way down.' (When de Quincey says, 'all the way down,' does he mean from the entire universe down through the sub atomic particles or waves.)?"

Thanks, my friend, for sharing the web site and comments. It all may be a bit confusing, and maybe a bit far out to extend the idea of consciousness to non-living things, but it's just the next big jump to do so. With a bit of imagination—which all fiction writers have—I simply extended it beyond humans and animals, to…well…who really knows? I was also inspired by the fact that many of Hans Christian Andersen's "fairy tales" are about everyday objects, so I am not the first author to have played with this idea.

The whole concept made me look around at some of my own things and think about their stories. As of this writing, Antique Clock still sits on my piano. I had to make up what may have happened before my grandparents bought it. I surely hope my children and grandchildren will make sure Antique Clock's story has a very different ending—that "he" will continue to tick-tock in the home of one of my descendants long after I leave this world.

I also want to thank the following people who provided information about items in pawn shops, pawn shop policies, and police procedures that I hope make this bit of fantasy more "believable" as I completed the first draft:

Sources:

Anthony Andrade, Cash America Pawn, 1020 Gessner Dr., Houston TX 77055

Gerardo Moreno at Half Price Pawn, 2038 Gessner Dr., Suite C, Houston TX 77080

Officer Castle, on duty for questions, Houston Police Department, Northwest Station Nov., 2014